False Faith

A Small-Town Mystery of Murder and Corruption

Anna Jackson

PART ONE

Chapter 1 – A Return to Ashwood

James Whitaker hadn't seen the town of Ashwood in nearly fifteen years, yet as he drove past the familiar bend where the highway narrowed into a tree-lined country road, he felt the years collapse in on themselves. The forest pressed close on either side, pine and maple interlocking like conspirators whispering overhead. Summer had deepened into its late stretch; the air was heavy with humidity, and roadside wildflowers tilted toward the fading evening light.

He gripped the wheel of his aging sedan, his reflection in the windshield catching a face both older and wearier than the one that had left Ashwood years before. He had chased stories across states and continents, scribbling notes in airports and late-night diners, but something in him had always remained unfinished. That may have been why Hannah's invitation struck such a chord.   The Whitaker estate rose from the trees like a relic of another century. The gray stone house, with its white trim and slate roof, had been built by his great-grandfather, once a symbol of old wealth and stubborn pride. In the years since, the family had sold much of the land. Still, the house remained a gathering place, restored and repurposed for weddings, community events, and tonight's celebration: Hannah's engagement.

James parked near the edge of the gravel drive, the crunch of stones beneath his tires pulling him back to childhood memories—racing bikes down the lane, chasing fireflies with

Hannah until their hands smelled of grass and sweat. He stepped out of the car and paused. Lanterns glowed across the lawn, strung from tree to tree and swaying gently in the warm breeze. Laughter drifted through the air, mingling with the soft notes of a string quartet playing on the veranda.

"James!"

Hannah rushed toward him in a pale blue dress, her auburn hair pinned in loose curls. She hugged him tightly, nearly knocking the overnight bag from his shoulder.

"You came! I wasn't sure you'd pull yourself away from whatever dangerous assignment you're chasing."

"No danger lately," James said with a smile. "Unless you count filing invoices on time."   A

"You look good," she said, squeezing his hands. "Tired, maybe—but good."

"So do you. Glowing, actually. Your fiancé must be treating you right."

Hannah blushed and tugged him toward the crowd. "Come on. I'll introduce you. Everyone's dying to meet the cousin I keep bragging about."

Inside, James shook hands with neighbors, distant relatives, and local officials. He offered polite smiles, but his reporter's instincts cataloged details automatically: who avoided eye contact, who watched others too closely, who drank more than they should. It was a reflex he couldn't turn off.

Daniel Harper, Hannah's fiancé, was tall and broad-shouldered, with the kind of handshake politicians practiced in mirrors. His smile was disarming, his voice steady, but James felt a faint unease. Maybe it was nothing more than the protectiveness of an older brother figure.

After the speeches and toasts, James slipped away toward the gardens, needing air. The estate grounds stretched behind the house in neat stone paths bordered by hedges and flowerbeds. The air smelled of lilacs and damp earth, a welcome reprieve from the crowded chatter inside.

The pavilion stood at the edge of the pond, its wooden frame painted white, lanterns dangling from its beams. From a distance, it looked peaceful—a perfect place for quiet reflection. But as James approached, something about the stillness unsettled him.

At first, he thought someone was resting there. A man sat on the bench, head bowed, one hand hanging loosely at his side. The position was too rigid, too unnatural. As James drew closer, dread tightened in his chest.

It was Charles Redmond.

Redmond was impossible to ignore in Ashwood—wealthy, commanding, the kind of man whose shadow seemed longer than the buildings he owned. James remembered him from boyhood fundraisers and civic meetings, always in control, always the loudest voice in the room. Now he was silent.

James crouched beside him. The man's tie was loosened, his jacket open. His skin, usually ruddy with temper and drink, had gone pale. James touched his wrist instinctively, but the absence of a pulse was immediate and final.

Then he noticed the details. The shattered glass of Redmond's wristwatch, spiderweb cracks spreading across its face. Faint bruises along his knuckles. And in the soil near the bench, a second set of footprints.

James straightened, his pulse quickening. This wasn't a natural death.

A sudden rustle behind him snapped his attention around. A flashlight beam cut across the pavilion floor, momentarily blinding him.

"Step back," a woman's voice ordered.

James blinked, raising his hands slightly. A tall figure approached, dark hair pulled back, a badge clipped at her hip. Her eyes—sharp, steady—swept over him before dropping to Redmond's body.

"Detective Elena Marquez," she said curtly. "And you are?"

"James Whitaker. I grew up here. He was already like this when I found him."

Her jaw tightened. She crouched, gloved hands moving with practiced efficiency as she checked Redmond's throat, his eyes, his pockets. She didn't waste time pretending to hope for a pulse.

James frowned. "How did you know to come here?"

She glanced up, the flashlight catching the hard line of her cheekbone. "An officer on perimeter patrol radioed in. Said he saw someone enter the gardens alone and didn't come out. When I heard Redmond's name, I decided to take a look myself." She let the words settle, then added, "Good thing I did."

James shifted uneasily. "So you expected to find a dead body waiting?"

Her eyes narrowed. "No. But I expected trouble. And I found it."

Before James could respond, voices carried from the path. More officers arrived, summoned by Elena's call. Uniforms moved briskly, securing the area with tape and quiet commands. Guests gathered at the edge of the lawn, whispers rippling through the crowd.

Hannah appeared with Daniel close behind, her face pale. "Oh no... James, what happened? Is that Charles?"

He opened his mouth, but Elena cut in. "Step back, ma'am. This is a crime scene now."

Daniel bristled. "With all due respect, Detective, Charles Redmond was a pillar of this community."

"And now he's dead," Elena said flatly. "So unless you want to contaminate evidence, you'll stay behind the line."

Murmurs spread like wildfire, the celebration dissolving into confusion. Some whispered theories; others clutched their children tighter. The string quartet had fallen silent. Only the buzz of voices and the occasional flash of a camera phone punctuated the night.

Elena rose from her crouch, fixing James with a look that weighed him like evidence on a scale. "Mr. Whitaker, you'll need to make a statement. But for now, I suggest you don't stray too far. Until I know exactly what happened here, I have to consider every possibility."

James swallowed hard. He had come back to Ashwood expecting nostalgia, laughter—maybe even a sense of belonging he hadn't felt in years. Instead, he stood at the edge of something darker. A story was unfolding around him, one he wasn't sure he wanted to be part of.

But from the way Detective Marquez's sharp, suspicious gaze lingered on him, he already knew he wouldn't be allowed to remain just a bystander.

Chapter 2 – Suspects and Secrets

Detective Elena Marquez moved with the quiet authority of someone who had long ago learned that calmness controlled a crowd better than shouting. Even as voices rose in panic across the Whitaker lawn, she gestured to her officers, and the chaos gave way to reluctant order. Yellow tape stretched across the garden path. Guests were corralled onto the veranda, murmuring furiously into their champagne glasses.

James sat on a wrought-iron chair near the pavilion, an officer hovering a few feet away to ensure he didn't wander. He watched Elena crouch once more beside Charles Redmond's body, her gloved hands working methodically, her dark eyes tracking every inch of the scene. She didn't miss a thing—or at least she gave no indication of it. She checked the broken crystal of Redmond's watch, noted the position of his hands, the faint abrasions across his knuckles, and the second set of footprints pressed into the soft earth. When she rose, a flicker of thought crossed her face and vanished just as quickly.

He should have felt relief. After all, this wasn't his story to write—not officially. But the journalist in him couldn't resist cataloging every detail. The cousin in him wanted to wish it all away, to rewind to speeches and laughter and the way Hannah had glowed by the veranda railing.

Elena approached him. "You said you found him like this?"

"Yes."

"Alone?"

James hesitated. He thought of the overlapping prints. "Yes. Alone."

Her eyes narrowed at the hitch in his voice. "You hesitated."

"I noticed footprints near the bench. Not mine."

She nodded without committing. "We'll see what forensics says. Officer Hale will take your statement. Don't leave the grounds."

James watched her stride away, her focus already shifting to the other guests. She was sharp, efficient, but there was an undercurrent beneath her composure—something that felt like suspicion aimed squarely at him.

The veranda had transformed into a holding area. Lantern light trembled over anxious faces as Elena began her questioning, one person at a time. The music stands looked abandoned, sheet music lifting at the corners as if trying to escape.

First came Margaret Redmond, Charles's estranged wife. She wore a black evening gown that would have looked theatrical at a celebration, if not for the way it fit her like armor. Her diamond necklace caught the light each time she lifted her chin.

"When was the last time you saw your husband alive?" Elena asked.

Margaret's painted lips curved into a bitter smile. "Charles and I haven't lived as husband and wife in any meaningful way for years, Detective. Tonight was courtesy and obligation. He came because appearances matter to him—even after he's burned through everything else."

"You argued with him."

"We always argued," Margaret said lazily, though the muscle in her jaw tightened. "About money, about his temper, about the pretty assistants who come and go. I spoke with him near the bar. He accused me of showing up to gloat. I told him if I wanted to gloat, I'd have brought the press."

"A timeline," Elena said. "From the bar to now."

Margaret flicked her wrist. "I spoke with Hannah. Then Daniel. Then Councilwoman Lila Enderly. She can confirm. I was inside when whatever happened to Charles happened."

James observed carefully. Margaret's tone was glassy with contempt, but her fingers kept drifting toward the base of her throat, worrying an invisible thread. For a woman who claimed not to care, she seemed rattled.

Next came Evan Carlisle, Charles's business partner. Evan was short and tightly wound, with a face that had learned to smile in boardrooms and now couldn't remember how. His tie was pulled too tight, and sweat dotted his hairline.

"I understand you were heard arguing with Mr. Redmond earlier this week," Elena said, her voice even.

"It was about business," Evan snapped. "He was impulsive. He promised investors he could cover shortfalls from a property sale that hasn't closed." He faltered. "I mean—a temporary liquidity issue. Charles knew how to swing big. He was going to land on his feet. He always did."

"Tonight?" Elena prompted.

"He told me to stop second-guessing him. Said after the engagement announcement, a benefactor would 'recommit.' I don't know what that means."

Elena let the word hang: benefactor. "Where were you at nine-thirty?"

Evan's pupils flicked left—the way people's eyes do when they consult memory... or fabricate it. "Inside. With Councilwoman Enderly and Mayor Trent. Check with them."

"Count on it," Elena said.

Then Hannah sat, hands smoothing her dress in an effort to still their shaking. Daniel hovered a step behind until Elena motioned him aside.

"Hannah," Elena said, her tone softening, "did you speak with Charles earlier?"

Hannah swallowed. "He was cruel. He said Daniel wasn't good enough. He said if I married him, I'd regret it."

"Did you argue?"

Tears brightened Hannah's eyes. "I told him it wasn't his business. He said it was everyone's business when money and reputation were involved."

Daniel stepped forward, voice steady, gaze direct. "She was with me after that. We spoke with several guests. We didn't go near the gardens."

"Did you and Charles discuss money?" Elena asked Hannah.

Hannah blinked. "Money? No. He just brought it up. He said some funding he'd promised Daniel might be reevaluated."

Elena wrote nothing. Sometimes silence recorded more than ink.

Officers swept the gardens with flashlights. The pond lay black and indifferent, the pavilion a pale shape at its edge. A uniform approached Elena carrying a torn scrap of purple fabric, the threads vivid under the lantern light.

"Where was this?" Elena asked.

"On the bench edge, Detective. Looks like it caught when someone stood up—or turned fast."

Another officer returned with a fountain pen, gold-trimmed and engraved with the initials C.R.

"Found where?" Elena asked.

"Under a hydrangea near the pavilion, ma'am. Not far from the path."

A third officer held up a tiny plastic vial. "Glass fragments from the watch face. There's a smear—it might be skin or something else."

"Bag and log it," Elena said. "No assumptions."

From where James sat, he caught a faint trace of perfume—powdery, old-fashioned, like violets. He remembered catching the same scent near the pavilion. He tried to place it: Margaret, perhaps, or Councilwoman Enderly, or even one of the catering staff.

A caterer. That thought snagged. Staff moved everywhere unnoticed. Staff saw and heard everything.

A woman in a cranberry apron hovered near the veranda steps, arms folded tight against the night.

James edged closer. "You working the event?" he asked, keeping his tone easy.

She nodded. "Joan. Head server."

"Did you see Charles Redmond head toward the gardens?"

Her eyes flicked to his, cautious. "He passed me twice. The second time, he wasn't steady. Kept looking over his shoulder."

"Was anyone with him?"

She hesitated. "A woman crossed the lawn a few minutes later. I noticed because of the shoes—sharp heels on grass. She nearly twisted her ankle on the stones."

"Do you remember what she wore?"

"Dark dress. And a scarf. Purple, I think. You don't see that shade much."

James felt something shift. "Did she come back the same way?"

Joan shook her head. "Not by me."

"Thank you," James said.

An officer stepped in, reminding him not to wander. He raised his hands and allowed himself to be guided back.

Across the tape, Councilwoman Lila Enderly spoke animatedly with an officer, her silver hair catching the lantern light. Mayor Trent hovered beside her, flushed and uneasy. Enderly caught James watching and offered a tight, unreadable smile.

James gave his statement an hour later, recounting events as clearly as he could—the garden, the body, the watch, the footprints, the scent of violets. He left out the purple scarf. For now.

When he finished, Elena returned. "You're a journalist," she said.

"I am."

"Then you know the value of sticking to what you can prove."

"I wrote it on page one of my notebook," James said. "Right after the part about not antagonizing the person with a badge."

A faint hint of amusement touched her expression. "You've already broken both rules."

"Old habits."

She studied him. "Your cousin's fiancé—how well do you know him?"

"I met him today."

Her gaze cooled. "Don't leave town, Mr. Whitaker."

"I wasn't planning to."

"Good."

He watched her go, unease settling in.

Later, Daniel approached him again, his tone carefully casual. "Rough night. The detective seems capable."

James glanced at his shoes. A faint smear of pond-gray mud edged the sole. "You didn't go near the pavilion?"

Daniel followed his gaze, then laughed lightly. "Helped a waiter earlier. Dropped tray. That's all."

"Of course," James said.

Daniel nodded and moved on.

Near midnight, the frenzy dulled into exhaustion. The body was gone. Guests drifted away. The house dimmed.

In the library, James removed his jacket. A folded note slipped free and landed at his feet.

He unfolded it.

Leave it alone, Whitaker.

The handwriting was jagged, hurried. The paper faintly scented—violets.

Someone had been close enough to slip it into his pocket.

Someone was watching him.

James looked out toward the dark garden. The pavilion light flickered once, then died.

"Not this time," he said quietly.

He folded the note carefully and tucked it away like evidence.

Outside, beyond the window, something shifted in the hedges—then stilled.

Chapter 3 – The First Misdirection

The morning after Charles Redmond's death dawned gray and reluctant. Fog drifted up from the pond, smothering the gardens in a low, rolling blanket that clung to hedges and benches like an accusation. Yellow police tape still circled the pavilion, limp in the damp breeze, its warning letters blurred by dew. The Whitaker estate, usually so grand, looked tired and unsettled, like a hostess worn down by her own party.

James sat on the veranda steps, holding a mug of coffee that had gone lukewarm in his hand. He hadn't managed more than a few hours of restless sleep, and his thoughts kept looping back to the same image: Charles Redmond's body, stiff and slumped, and the fractured watch face frozen at nine-seventeen. Worse than the corpse itself was the note now folded in his wallet. *Leave it alone, Whitaker.* Whoever had written it hadn't just known his name. They had slipped the warning into his jacket pocket without his noticing, which meant they had been standing close enough to touch him during the chaos.

The estate felt different in daylight. The laughter and music of the night before were gone, replaced by the murmur of voices, the shuffle of uniformed officers combing the grounds, and the occasional snap of a camera flash. The fog muted everything, dulling edges and swallowing sound. James thought of how quickly joy had soured into dread. Ashwood had always been a town that prized appearances, but the thin layer of polish was already cracking. By now, gossip would be moving faster than any official report.

"Still brooding?" Hannah's voice startled him. She joined him on the step, a shawl wrapped around her shoulders, her hair unpinned and tumbling loose. Her face looked pale, her eyes raw from lack of sleep. "They're still here," she whispered, glancing toward the gardens where officers were photographing footprints.

"They'll be here until Elena has what she needs," James said.

"Detective Marquez." Hannah spoke the name with a shiver. "She doesn't believe me, James. I can see it in her eyes."

"She doesn't believe anyone yet," James said firmly. "That's her job."

Hannah stared into her lap, twisting the edge of her shawl. "I keep hearing his voice. The way he said Daniel wasn't good enough. The way I snapped back. It was the last thing he ever heard from me. I might as well have put a knife in his chest."

James set his mug aside and covered her hand with his. "Don't say that. He was alive when you walked away. That's the truth, and we're holding on to it."

Her eyes glistened, but she nodded.

By midmorning, Detective Elena Marquez gathered a small group in the dining room: Hannah, Daniel, Margaret Redmond, and Evan Carlisle. James wasn't invited, but he lingered in the hall outside, where the heavy oak door stood cracked just enough for voices to carry. He told himself it was loyalty that kept him there, but he knew better. It was the same restless instinct that had driven him into journalism years ago. The truth pulled at him, even when it burned.

Elena's voice came steady and calm. "We believe Mr. Redmond died sometime between nine and nine-thirty. The watch suggests nine-seventeen, but we'll wait on the medical examiner before declaring anything definitive. There are signs of a struggle. Abrasions on the hands. Bruising on the jaw. No weapon yet. Until we have more, I won't speculate."

Margaret Redmond let out a brittle laugh. "Speculation is all this town does. Half of Ashwood has already decided I poisoned him. The other half says Hannah pushed him into the pond."

"Stop it," Hannah said sharply, her voice cracking.

Elena's tone snapped like a whip. "Mrs. Redmond. Miss Whitaker. This is not a courtroom, and it is not a gossip parlor. Keep your remarks to the questions."

Chairs scraped. James leaned closer.

"Miss Whitaker," Elena continued, "you argued with Charles last night. You told me he threatened to withdraw support for Daniel's venture."

"Yes," Hannah whispered.

"Did he threaten you directly?"

"No. Charles used words like knives, but he didn't raise his hands. He wanted to scare me into compliance, not bruise me."

"Still, you argued. Witnesses saw you upset." Elena paused. "We found a piece of fabric at the scene. Purple, torn. It matches the scarf you were wearing earlier."

Hannah gasped. "That's not possible. I lost it hours earlier—I thought I left it in the ladies' room."

"Yet there it was," Elena said. "Caught on the bench where Charles died."

Daniel's voice cut in, sharp with anger. "Detective, Hannah was with me after that argument. Dozens of people saw us together."

Evan Carlisle gave a derisive snort. "If half the room was staring at you two mooning over each other, maybe that explains why nobody noticed Charles getting murdered outside."

"Enough," Elena snapped. The room fell silent.

The dining room door opened suddenly, and Hannah rushed past, her face blotched with tears. Daniel followed, his arm protective around her shoulders. James caught her before she could flee up the stairs.

"She thinks I killed him," Hannah whispered, her voice breaking. "She thinks I killed Charles."

"Then we'll prove you didn't," James said.

Elena appeared in the doorway behind them. "You heard enough," she said flatly.

"More than enough," James replied, his jaw tight.

"Then you know why your cousin remains a person of interest."

"She lost her scarf," James countered. "That doesn't mean she left it at the scene. Someone could have planted it."

"That's a possibility," Elena admitted. "But she lied to me once already. She said she went straight inside, when in fact she stopped in the restroom. That gap matters."

"You're reaching."

"You're protecting her. Understandable, but not useful." Her voice cooled. "Stay out of this, Whitaker."

"Can't," James said. "Family comes first."

Elena studied him for a long moment before turning on her heel, the sound of her footsteps echoing through the hall.

Later, James walked the grounds. The police had packed up most of their markers, but the earth still bore traces of their work, bright smudges of chalk dust and scraps of flagging tape left behind like scars. The pavilion loomed pale in the fog, its white paint ghostly against the pond.

He crouched by the bench. The soil was scuffed with so many overlapping tracks that they resembled a storm frozen in dirt. But one impression caught his attention: a knee print, pressed deep near the bench leg. If Charles had struggled, maybe someone had forced him down.

James scanned the area again. Something metallic glinted beneath a hydrangea bush several feet away. Pushing back the leaves, he found a cigarette butt—sleek, black-wrapped, an expensive brand he hadn't seen in years. Redmond had quit smoking ages ago. Someone else had been here.

He wrapped it in a handkerchief and slipped it into his pocket.

"Find something worth keeping?"

The voice made him start. Margaret Redmond stood on the path, a crystal glass of sherry in her hand, though it was barely past noon. She wore a dressing gown as though she had no intention of leaving the estate all day. Her smile was sharp, all teeth and no warmth.

"You think I killed him," she said coolly.

"I think Charles made enemies," James said carefully.

"Enemies keep their distance. Only family cuts close enough to bleed you." She sipped her drink and walked away, her heels crunching on the gravel.

James watched her retreat, unsettled. Her words weren't a confession, but they clung to him like smoke.

By evening, the fog had burned off. James returned to his rented room above the café in town, the creak of the stairs familiar beneath his weight. He placed the cigarette butt on the desk beside the folded warning note. Two clues, two shadows of intent, and nothing yet to connect them.

He sat down, meaning to write out what he knew, but the words refused to come. He rubbed his temples, listening to the muffled life below: clinking dishes, chairs scraping, bursts of laughter. Ordinary sounds in a town already darkened.

A knock jolted him upright. He opened the door cautiously. No one lingered in the hall, but on the floor lay a plain envelope.

He picked it up. Inside was a single sheet of paper. The handwriting was the same jagged scrawl as before:

Family won't protect you. Stop digging.

James sank into the chair, the paper trembling in his hand. Whoever was behind this wasn't just warning him now. They were threatening Hannah too.

He looked at the cigarette butt, the torn scarf, and the note. Pieces of a puzzle, arranged to point straight at his cousin. Someone wanted Hannah framed. Someone wanted him silenced.

James leaned back, staring at the ceiling beams. He could walk away. He could pack his bag that night, drive until Ashwood was nothing more than a bad dream in his rearview mirror. But he already knew he wouldn't.

He thought of Hannah at the dining room table, voice breaking. He thought of the fog over the pond, curling like a shroud. And he thought of Charles Redmond's lifeless eyes, fixed on nothing, as if death had stolen not only his breath but his secrets too.

No, James decided. He wasn't leaving this alone. Whoever had written those words had no idea how stubborn a Whitaker could be.

Chapter 4 – A Trail of Lies

Rain had continued through the night, slicking the pavement of Main Street and beading along the strip of purple fabric tied neatly to James's car antenna.

As was his habit since all the trouble started, and before going to bed, James went outside to assess the area. He stood in the narrow alley beside Mae's Café and removed the fabric. It felt heavy in his hand, another piece of evidence that wanted to be mistaken for Hannah's scarf. The windshield bore the starburst crack of a center punch—the kind a practiced hand makes. Not an angry smash, but a precise hit that weakens without shattering. That deliberate restraint chilled James more than raw vandalism would have. Rage breaks things. Intent leaves threats.

Mae appeared behind him, umbrella angled so the rain didn't soak the back of his neck. Her presence was quiet, natural—like someone who had learned how to stand witness without being asked.

"Purple again," she said, eyeing the strip in his fingers.

"It wants to be Hannah's," James replied. He turned the fabric over, tracing the cheap stitching. "Wrong weave. Wrong thread. But from three steps back, no one would know or care."

Mae exhaled through her nose, unimpressed. "You going to tell Elena?"

"Already did," James said, nodding toward the cruiser idling at the mouth of the alley. "She's here. She's deciding whether this is vandalism or a frame."

Detective Elena Marquez crossed the wet gravel with her coat collar turned up, her hands buried deep in her pockets. She took the fabric from James, weighing it the way she had weighed the scarf near the pavilion. Then she examined the cracked windshield.

"Camera?" she asked.

"Blind spot," James said. "Of course."

"They know your habits," she murmured. "Know you park under the light because you think it's safer."

She gave the faintest twitch of a smile—not humor, but acknowledgment. Then she slipped the fabric into an evidence bag. "I'll run it to the lab. Chain of custody, in case you worry I'll swap it for Hannah's scarf behind your back. Go upstairs. Sleep."

Sleep didn't come easily, even above Mae's café, where the air smelled faintly of coffee and cinnamon that never entirely faded. The room was small, with bare pine floors, a narrow bed, and a desk tucked beneath the window. James had grown to appreciate its simplicity. It was home without being sentimental, shelter without distraction. Yet that night, the shadows along the ceiling seemed to shift with every gust of wind rattling the glass.

When morning pushed gray light through the curtains, James descended the back stairs into Mae's kitchen. She was already at the stove, frying bacon with the radio muttering low. Hannah sat at the counter with a mug of tea she hadn't touched, her eyes hollow from another sleepless night.

"They came again," she said as soon as she saw him. "More questions. About the scarf. About whether I've ever loaned it to anyone."

"Do you own more than one?" James asked.

Hannah pressed her lips together. "One. Just one. But apparently, in this town, that's enough to make it sprout legs and tie itself around everything."

Mae set down a plate of toast in front of her. "Eat," she said.

"I can't."

"You will." Mae's voice brooked no argument. Hannah obeyed, picking up a slice with trembling hands.

Later, at the Redmond estate, the study smelled of polished wood and stale dust—the kind of room meant to intimidate visitors with its permanence. Charles Redmond's ledgers sat open on the desk. Elena was already there, sleeves rolled, her hair tied back, leaning over the numbers as if they might confess under her gaze.

"He was bleeding money," she said when James entered. "Borrowing from himself, masking losses with creative labels."

"Evan's shells?" James asked, stepping closer.

Elena nodded. "Elm Tree Holdings, Phoenix Capital Partners, and Dead River, LLC. All smoke and mirrors. Evan didn't invent them; he learned from Charles—badly. We pulled statements. Charles borrowed from himself with interest. Evan managed the movements."

James scanned the columns. "Could Evan have killed him to cover it up?"

"Motive's not that simple," Elena replied. "Sometimes you kill a partner to hide a crime. Sometimes you keep him alive because he's the only one who knows how to juggle the knives. Evan doesn't strike me as a juggler."

"Or a killer," James added, though he wasn't sure she heard him.

By midday, Daniel appeared, storming into the study like he owned it. Hannah's fiancé radiated impatience, his tie askew, his words sharp. "You can't keep dragging this out," he snapped. "Hannah's being hounded. The town's eating her alive."

"She's not the center of this investigation," Elena said evenly. "She's a suspect. She's also my responsibility. That means we move carefully."

Daniel's gaze darted to James. "You're feeding this, aren't you? Writing your little notes, making her look guilty?"

James didn't flinch. "Someone wants her framed. That's not me."

"You accusing me?"

"I'm accusing the person who thought purple was close enough," James said. "If that's you, confess to having a bad eye for color."

Daniel's jaw flexed. He looked like he wanted to swing, but Elena's presence froze him in place. Finally, he shoved his hands into his pockets and left without another word.

James had doubts about Evan's part in Charles Redmond's death.

He sought Denise, Evan's assistant, and she agreed to meet with him at a table near the back of Mae's cafe. She arrived with a folder, sat, and placed it between them. "Minutes," she said. "Board meetings. Not all official. Some less official."

Inside were photocopies of single-page minutes. Charles's tidy initials appeared in margins beside phrases like capital release and bridge facility. Evan's name appeared as E.C., with arrows that led nowhere.

"Evan copied Charles's tricks badly," she said. "That's what makes it so easy to make him look like the villain now. He doesn't know how to conceal his flaws. Charles did."

"And if Evan didn't kill Charles?"

"Then the person who did knew Evan would fit the story the town wanted," she said. "Evan tried to copy Charles and nearly choked. He's guilty of desperation, not murder."

James lowered his pen. "Where was he when Charles was killed?"

Her lips tightened. "With me. In the office. Not working."

"Why not tell the police?"

"Because," she said flatly. "Detective Marquez doesn't want to hear it. She wants this case closed."

The lab results arrived that afternoon. Elena put the call on speaker.

"Purple fiber from Whitaker lot," the analyst reported. "Polyester blend, commercial fabric, common retail scarf. No DNA. Doesn't match Hannah Moore's scarf. Auto scrap smells faintly of automotive grease; Hannah's scarf smells like cedar. It's a plant."

"Poorly planted," Elena corrected. "Whoever staged it doesn't shop where Hannah shops."

"Or they wore gloves."

"Hannah's scarf is clean," James added. "Whoever tied the fabric to my antenna used a solvent that doesn't live in her closet."

"She'll be relieved to know her closet has been exonerated," Elena said. "I don't think she did it."

Relief hit him hard, and he surprised himself by saying, "You won't say that out loud."

"I just did," she replied. "But not where it will be typed. The town deserves careful truth. I'll move quietly. Evan's books smell wrong."

By late afternoon, a new rumor was circulating. Charles had been bankrupt in spirit and in ledger, and Evan had been the student who had poorly learned enough to get caught. That rumor suited Ashwood.

James took his notebook back to his room and laid out two columns: *What looks like guilt* and *What is guilt.* Under the first, he wrote: shells, argument, scarf, pen. Under the second: money that evaporates; a punch that stops before it finishes; a town hungry for relief.

He was still staring at the lists when his phone chimed. A text from an unknown number.

Leave it alone.

Attached was a photo of his cracked windshield from the night before, the purple fabric still tied in place, rain streaking across the glass. Taken up close. Too close.

James's pulse quickened. Someone was watching him. He texted back one word.

No.

No response came.

At 10:15 p.m., Elena called. "Tomorrow morning I'm filing a request for a warrant on Evan's devices and accounts. I'll have it by noon."

"You're going to arrest him?"

"I'm going to arrest him. There's enough evidence for him to sit in a cell while I test whether the rest is true," she said. "He's guilty of purposely mishandling financial reports, if not murder."

The next morning, the courthouse hummed with anticipation. James leaned against the lamppost outside Mae's, sipping coffee she had forced into his hand, and watched the crowd gathering on the steps. The whispers carried the same refrain: Evan Carlisle. They've got him. It's over.

James shook his head. Convenient. Too convenient.

If Elena arrested Evan Carlisle today, the town would exhale in satisfaction.

Chapter 5 – The Convenient Suspect

Ashwood woke to a rumor already half believed. By seven, the regulars at Mae's were speaking of certainty the way they talked about weather. By eight, the word arrest floated over Main Street like a banner. By nine, James stood at the café window with his coffee cooling in his hand and watched townspeople turn their faces toward the courthouse, drawn by curiosity.

He climbed to his room above the café, the steps creaking a rhythm he knew as well as his heartbeat. On the desk, his notes from the night before lay open. There were columns of debts and names. He slid the notebook into his jacket and headed back down, the smell of coffee and butter following him.

By late morning, the courthouse steps had become chaotic. By noon, a line of microphones bloomed from stands that weren't there at nine, creating a makeshift press area. Freelancers from two counties over pressed elbows with a TV anchor whose perfect hair defied humidity. James took his place with the rest, not because he believed in announcements, but because public performances reveal what private conversations conceal.

The heavy door opened, and Detective Elena Marquez stepped into the light. Her suit was plain and dark; her posture made opinions unnecessary. Two uniforms flanked her, both stone-faced and young enough to want this moment to be history.

"Good morning," Elena said, no microphone needed. "This morning, Evan Carlisle was taken into custody on suspicion of the murder of Charles Redmond. Our investigation uncovered financial fraud tied to Mr. Redmond's companies and Mr. Carlisle's shell entities. Witness accounts place Mr. Carlisle near the Whitaker estate on the night of the murder. He had motive, access, and opportunity."

Murmurs broke like a small surf. Relief traveled faster than air. Cameras clicked a congregation's amen.

"We believe the arrest is supported by evidence," she said, and stepped back.

The town exhaled. Ashwood loved an official verb, and arrested was one of its favorites. People drifted toward Mae's with talk that tasted like closure.

James stayed on the courthouse lawn, watching the door, until a small convoy rolled from the side lot. First a cruiser, then a transport with Evan Carlisle behind glass, head down, hands hidden. Denise stood across the street, half shadowed by a lamppost, her face white as paper. When the transport turned onto Main, her knees buckled and she fell.

James threaded through the dispersing crowd, reached her side, and helped her up. "Tell me I'm wasting my time," he said quietly. "Tell me he could have been anywhere but where you were at the proposed time of Charles's death."

Her jaw moved once. "I'm done hiding for a man who never learned how to hide himself," she said. "But I won't say it here."

"Mae's," he said. "Fifteen minutes."

She nodded and walked quickly away.

Inside Mae's, the television above the pie case played a silent loop of Elena at the microphones while captions paraphrased certainty. Denise slid into the rear booth, hands flat on the table the way people place them before a palm reader. James sat opposite and opened his notebook.

"Okay," he said. "Tell me again where he was."

"In his office," she answered, meeting his eyes. "With me. We were not working."

"You understand what saying that aloud does," he said.

"It ruins us," she said. "But letting him sit in a cell for a murder he didn't commit would ruin me more."

"Why not tell Elena this morning?"

"She already had her script," Denise said. "She needed the arrest to stand. If I walked up there with the truth, the town would call it spite."

She slid a printout across the table. It contained door swipes, camera thumbnails, and an entry that read BOARD PREP 7:30–9:30. The thumbnails were grainy but unmistakable: Evan in shirtsleeves entering the inner office at eight-oh-six, and no sign of him leaving again until after nine.

"What about the witness?" James asked.

"Mrs. Delaney on North Ferry," Denise said, rubbing her temples. "She sees a tan coat and a man with dark hair every night and calls it Evan. He and half of Ashwood own tan coats."

James wrote: Delaney—habit, not fact. Then: Affair = alibi. He drew a box around both words as if a pencil could build a shelter. "Will you swear it?"

She swallowed. "If it keeps him from being tried for a murder he didn't commit, yes."

He found Elena at the station, the lobby humming with the bureaucratic equivalent of a beehive—printers whirring, phones ringing, and a receptionist who sharpened every "please hold" like a blade. Elena stood near the bullpen window, reading a file.

"Talk privately?" James asked.

"Thirty seconds," she said, leading him to a quiet corner where the paint had dulled and the clock ran a minute slow.

"Evan has an alibi," James said. "Denise was with him. Calendar logs back it up."

Elena's stare didn't blink. "She'll put it in writing?"

"She will."

"Your 'calendar logs' will survive scrutiny?"

"Badge swipes and thumbnails. None of them read love; all of them read presence."

Elena looked past him, then back, measuring. "We booked him on probable cause," she said. "Not certainty. If her statement holds, I pivot. I won't do it from the steps."

"You did the arrest from the steps," he said. "Do the correction from there too."

Her jaw set, not with anger but resolve. "I'll do what keeps me from losing two cases," she said. "Bring me the printout and a written statement."

He nodded, already turning, already dialing Denise.

Afternoon slunk in under a ceiling of clouds. James paced the alley behind Mae's while Denise, in his room, typed, printed, and signed. He could hear the ritual through the open window. When she handed him the statement, her fingers shook. He slid it into a folder.

"Elena won't thank you," he said.

"I'm not fishing for thanks," Denise said. "I'm trying to teach this town the difference between relief and truth."

He was halfway to the station when his phone buzzed. Hannah: *Are they letting Evan go?* He typed: *Working on it.* A moment later: *James, be careful.* He wanted to say he didn't know how. Instead he wrote: *Always.*

He went to the station to meet Elena. She intercepted him before the desk sergeant could decide what kind of obstacle to become. He handed her the statement. She scanned it, flipped it, scanned it again, then passed it to the sergeant. "Photocopy, file, timestamp," she said. Then, to James: "Come with me."

In the corridor she didn't slow. "If this stands," she said, "I can't hold Evan on the murder without more. I can hold him on financial fraud while I pull at the rest."

They didn't reach her office. A call hissed from the nearest phone cradle. A uniform grabbed it, listened, paled, and turned. "Detective," he said, voice too loud in the wrong place. "We have a 10-54 at Redmond House."

Elena didn't ask what 10-54 meant. She moved. James moved with her because there are people you shadow when the world tips.

The Redmond house wore grief. Upstairs, the bathroom door hung open at the hinge stop.

Margaret lay in the tub, the water drained to a slick gloss, hair fanned out, skin pale with the particular stillness that follows the stopping of a heart. A glass rested on the vanity, its rim painted with a smear of lipstick. A pill bottle sat nearby, cap askew and a bottle of lavender bath oil remained open. The bath mat lay crooked, like a rug tugged and left that way by someone who ran out of time.

James stood at the threshold and swallowed the sound in his throat. Elena edged past the CSU tech, eyes scanning, slow and merciless. She looked at the wrists. No bruising. No marks on the shoulders. The rim of the tub was clean except for a faint trace where water had carried a faint purple stain.

"This wasn't suicide," James said, his voice low enough to belong to the tile. "It's staged."

The house filled with the mechanics of the aftermath. Photographs were taken. Gloves were worn to protect evidence. Fingerprints were dusted, and items were sealed in bags.

Downstairs, a neighbor cried into a tissue printed with daisies. Daniel paced like a man who had lost his place and couldn't find it again. Hannah sat rigid, hand in Mae's, eyes fixed on nothing.

James crouched beside Hannah's chair. "Tell me how you found her."

"Mrs. Larkin has a spare key," Hannah said, her words scraped raw. "Margaret didn't answer her phone. I called Mae. Mae said to call Elena. I knocked. I didn't want to go in alone. Mrs. Larkin came. I wish she hadn't."

"You didn't touch anything?"

"No," she said, with a small, fierce sort of pride. "I remembered what you always said about that."

He squeezed her shoulder and stood. Daniel intercepted him at the archway, jaw flexing, breath hot with coffee and anger. "This is your fault," he hissed. "You and your journalistic questions."

On the porch, Elena stood in the sickly light, rain just beginning to tap the rail. "If I cut Evan loose," she said without preamble, "this town eats me alive for a day. If I don't, the right person keeps breathing easy. Choose my headline."

"Neither," James said. "Choose your evidence."

She pinched the bridge of her nose, then dropped her hand. "I'll keep him on the fraud. I'll call the ME for a rush. I'll pull pharmacy records, phone logs, and every camera between here and the square. And I'll stand up tomorrow and say nothing dramatic."

"You'll have to say something," he said.

"I'll say the investigation is ongoing," she replied. "And mean it."

He walked home through the rain. The room above Mae's held its quiet like a friend. He set his wet jacket over the chair, opened his notebook, and wrote: *Evan arrested; alibi credible; Margaret dead—drowned by design; planted scene.* His phone vibrated against the tabletop. Unknown number.

Leave it alone.

No photo this time. He stared at the message until the words went soft around the edges, then turned the phone facedown.

"Eat," Mae said from the doorway, not a question. She set a bowl of stew on the desk and rested her hand on his shoulder for a second. "You look like a man who keeps running into locked doors. Keys show up after you sleep."

"I don't sleep," he said.

"Then close your eyes and pretend," she said. "It fools your body enough to keep you from falling over."

When she was gone, he ate because she had told him to, and because eating was a rebellion against the part of him that enjoyed martyrdom. He washed the bowl, went back to the desk, and drew the map again. This time he wrote in the corner: *Who benefits from Evan in a cell? From Margaret gone? From the town's relief?* He didn't have a name.

At ten, Elena called. "ME estimates time of death between seven and eight. The level of sedatives is inconsistent with voluntary use. No water in the lungs sufficient to suggest she fell asleep. We're treating it as homicide."

"Margaret wouldn't choose lavender and pills," James said. "She'd choose a stage and applause."

He sat a long time after the line went dead, listening to the café's last dishes settle below and the rain worry the eaves. When he finally undressed, it was like pulling off a costume that had stuck to his skin.

Morning came gray and damp, and with it the consequence of public opinion. The town wanted Elena to be certain. The town wanted James to be quiet. The town wanted anything but this new murder. He carried his coffee to the window and watched people choose sides with their shoulders.

Hannah texted: *I dreamed Margaret sat up and asked if anyone had picked up her dry cleaning. I woke up and hated her for leaving me with a dream that stupid. Is that allowed?* He typed: *Yes.* She replied: *Find who did this.* He wrote: *Trying.*

At nine, he walked to the station with Denise's sworn statement in his folder and a sentence he hated in his mouth: We have the wrong man. He didn't know whether he would say it to Elena or to the town or to his own notes.

Outside the station, the same young officer from yesterday stood with a clipboard, face raw with having slept in a chair. He nodded to James now, terse—an acknowledgment that men who keep showing up are either fools or necessary. Inside, Elena was already moving, already building a day out of phone calls and quiet orders. She saw the folder in his hand and lifted hers in answer. Two files, two paths, one town.

"Mr. Whitaker," she said, and this time there was something like respect buried under the professional gravel, "we're going to reopen the timeline."

"I'll walk it with you," he said.

"We'll walk different sides of the street," she replied, "and meet in the middle when we have to."

"Fair."

She glanced at the clock. "Go write what you have to write," she said. "But leave me room to be right later."

"I can do that," he said.

He stepped back into the rain, tasted metal in the air, and knew the chapter was closing itself without his permission. Evan Carlisle sat in a cell for crimes he may or may not have committed. Margaret Redmond lay in a tub drained of water and dignity.

James turned toward Mae's, toward the stairs, intending to write more in his notebook. The bell on the café door chimed, a sound his bones recognized before his ears did. He paused at the landing and listened to voices finding their tables, to spoons touching ceramic, to the town rehearsing normal. Then he climbed, sat, opened the notebook, and wrote the line that hurt: *We arrested the wrong man.*

He underlined it twice, closed the cover, and stared out at the rain. Breathing in coffee and damp brick, he braced himself for what was coming next, whether anyone wanted it or not.

Chapter 6 – Shadows of the Past

Ashwood carried grief the way its trees carried moss—quietly, clinging, never letting go. After Margaret Redmond's drowning, the townsfolk carried on. Children still hurried to school with damp hair, and shopkeepers still rolled up their awnings every morning. Customers at Mae's Café drank their coffee in unusual silence, eyes darting toward the door whenever it opened. Everyone knew the truth: one death might be misfortune, but two deaths meant something darker.

James Whitaker had grown up in this town, and he recognized the feeling. It was the same tone Ashwood had carried years ago when a factory fire had killed two men and left a dozen unemployed. Everyone had whispered then too, blaming men for being careless, deciding guilt before the investigation was complete. It had later turned out to be arson, and the guilty party had been caught, convicted, and sent to prison.

From his room above Mae's, James could smell frying bacon, hear the creak of chairs on the café floorboards, the soft scrape of spoons, and the pauses in conversation when his name was mentioned. He leaned over his desk, notebook open, and reread the words he had scrawled across the top of the page: *We arrested the wrong man. Who profits here?*

The arrest of Evan Carlisle had been swift—too swift—and the town had swallowed it like medicine. Elena Marquez had stood on the courthouse steps with all the authority of law behind her, declaring Carlisle guilty before most people had even learned the details. But Margaret's death had complicated that conclusion.

James tapped the end of his pen against the page. Margaret had been silenced, or at least removed, before she could say too much. And if Evan had an alibi, which James was certain he did, then the real killer was still out there—patient and careful.

The Redmond estate felt different now that Margaret was gone. Without her sharp voice echoing through its halls, the house seemed unusually quiet. Officers worked methodically, boxing documents and cataloging possessions. The study smelled of dust, leather, and stale cigar smoke, the air heavy with the residue of Charles Redmond.

Elena stood at the desk with her sleeves rolled, her hair pulled back, and her jaw set. A thick ledger lay open in front of her, the columns of numbers dense and uncompromising.

"You keep turning up in places you don't belong," she said as James entered.

"And you keep tolerating it," James answered. He crossed to the desk, eyeing the ledger. "What's caught your eye?"

Elena's lips pressed together. "Don't mistake tolerance for permission."

"Noted," he said. "What have you found?"

"Debts," Elena replied flatly. "Charles borrowed from himself, shuffled money between accounts like shells on a table. He was clever. Too clever for his own good."

James lifted another folder from the desk and thumbed through it. It contained contracts, promissory notes, and land deeds. "Clever isn't the word I'd use. Ruthless fits better. These aren't just deals. They're traps." The contracts were all signed by Charles

Redmond. At first glance, they were for construction projects, land acquisitions, and loans. But as he read further, patterns began to emerge—deals struck on unfair terms, promises broken, small businesses absorbed. "Charles wasn't just wealthy. He was ruthless."

Elena gave him a sideways glance. "Explain."

James laid out a document. "Here he loaned a farmer money at twenty percent interest. The farmer defaults, and Charles acquires the land. He holds it for a year, sells to a developer, and triples his profit. He destroyed a family to make a few thousand more."

Elena's eyes narrowed as she scanned the page. "And the farmer becomes another enemy."

"Multiply that by a dozen families, a dozen businesses, and you've got half the town with motive to kill him," James said.

Elena leaned back. "So what? Do we drag in every ruined farmer and bankrupt shopkeeper? You know as well as I do that motive isn't enough. Plenty of people hated Charles Redmond. Only one of them killed him."

James studied her. "That's true. But if someone went to the trouble of framing Hannah and Evan, it wasn't random. It was someone who wanted control. Charles was the puppet master when he was alive. His killer wants to play that role now."

They worked in silence for another hour, each sifting through stacks of papers. James began to notice a pattern of initials scattered in the margins of certain documents. They were cryptic notations that didn't seem to belong to Charles. He was about to ask Elena when his hand brushed against the underside of a drawer.

Something was taped there.

He crouched, tugging carefully until the adhesive gave way. A yellowed envelope slid free, its paper brittle with age. Inside was a folded letter. The handwriting was bold. The ink had faded, but it was still legible.

Charles, it read. Your debts are no longer yours alone. If you wish to keep what little dignity remains, you will do as instructed. Blackmail is an ugly word, but it keeps men honest. We are partners in this, though you will never admit it aloud. Payment is expected. Failure will be costly.

At the bottom were two initials.

James's stomach tightened. Initials. Not a name, just enough to taunt.

"Elena," he called.

She leaned over his shoulder, reading quickly. Her face remained expressionless, but her fingers tightened slightly against the edge of the desk.

"Blackmail," she murmured. "A partner. Initials instead of a name."

"Which means this letter is a key," James said. "The killer may not be someone who just hated Charles. It may have been someone who worked with him."

Elena folded the letter carefully and slid it into an evidence sleeve. "Initials won't get us far. A defense attorney would laugh this out of court."

"Maybe," James said. "In Ashwood, initials are everything. Someone in this town will recognize them."

Her gaze sharpened. "Not yet. We share this with the wrong person, we lose our advantage."

James tilted his head. "So you don't trust your team?"

"I trust results," Elena answered.

Back in his room above Mae's, the initials burned into him. He scribbled a list of names. *Carlisle. Harper. Larkin. Redmond. Whitaker.* None fit neatly, but the possibilities gnawed at him.

Mae knocked softly before stepping in, a plate balanced on one hand. "You'll starve before you solve anything," she said, setting down stew and bread.

James glanced up. "Thanks."

Her eyes flicked to the names. "That looks like trouble."

"Old trouble," James said.

"Old trouble is still trouble," Mae replied. "Be careful where you dig."

She left him to the silence, and James ate mechanically, his thoughts still on the initials and the blackmail, the debts, the hidden partner. He flipped to a clean page in his notebook and scrawled a new question in bold: *WHO HELD THE STRINGS?*

The next afternoon, James drove out of town. The need for fresh air had gnawed at him all morning. He told himself he would clear his head by retracing some of Charles's business deals, maybe stop at old farms or shuttered shops that still bore his fingerprints.

The county roads stretched long and empty, lined with bare trees that swayed against the gray sky. James tapped his fingers against the steering wheel, rehearsing questions. He imagined talking to Mr. Bailey, whose hardware store Charles had bought and gutted. Or the Donnelly family, forced off their land after Charles foreclosed on them. Each name was another shadow in Charles's past.

But then James noticed something in his rearview mirror.

A dark sedan, three lengths back. At first, he dismissed it as a coincidence. But when he slowed at a curve, the sedan slowed too. When he turned onto a narrower road, the sedan followed.

James's grip tightened on the wheel.

This wasn't a coincidence. Someone was following him.

James pressed harder on the accelerator, his car jolting forward as gravel spat beneath the tires. The sedan behind him matched his pace, unwavering. His pulse drummed in his ears, the steady rhythm of adrenaline urging him to act.

He took the next bend faster than he should have, the trees whipping past in a blur of gray and brown. The sedan rounded the curve seconds later, closing the distance like a predator confident its prey couldn't escape.

James's mind worked furiously. He was no stranger to danger. His years as a freelance journalist had put him in back alleys with smugglers, on picket lines with strikebreakers, and once in a warehouse in Boston where he had narrowly avoided a fist that could have broken his jaw. But being stalked on a country road outside Ashwood felt different. This was personal.

He eased off the gas, hoping the sedan would pass, but instead it surged forward, drawing up alongside him. James caught a glimpse of the driver—a shape more than a face, hidden behind the glare of glass. The car swerved, nudging dangerously close to his fender.

The ditch loomed to his right, deep and jagged, a tumble of rocks waiting to tear the undercarriage apart. James gritted his teeth and jerked the wheel left, bumping the sedan's door with a sharp clang of metal. The other driver retaliated, forcing him closer to the edge.

For one terrible second, his tires slipped, half the car tilting toward the ravine. His stomach lurched as the world tipped sideways. He yanked the wheel back, the car fishtailing wildly. Gravel spat like shrapnel. Somehow, mercifully, the tires caught.

He regained the road, heart pounding so hard he thought it might split his ribs. The sedan didn't slow. It roared ahead, then braked hard, attempting to cut him off entirely. James swerved again, his side mirror snapping against a tree. The impact jarred his arm to the shoulder.

Then, as suddenly as it had started, the sedan veered away. It accelerated down a side road and disappeared into the woods, its taillights vanishing like the last flare of a match.

James slowed to a crawl, pulling onto the shoulder. He sat gripping the wheel, breath ragged, sweat cold against the back of his neck. The ticking of the engine filled the silence, mocking the thunder in his chest.

Whoever had been behind that wheel hadn't wanted to scare him. They had wanted him gone.

He stayed parked for nearly ten minutes, regaining control of his breathing. Every instinct screamed at him to turn back, to head straight into Ashwood and lock his door behind him. But fear wasn't his trade. Stories didn't reveal themselves to men who flinched.

James eased back onto the road, driving slowly now, his eyes flicking to the rearview mirror at every turn. The woods pressed close on either side, their shadows heavy, but the sedan didn't return. Whoever had followed him had given up—for now.

By the time he reached Ashwood, dusk had begun to settle. He parked behind the café, climbed the narrow staircase, and dropped heavily into the chair at his desk. His hands still trembled as he set down his notebook.

He stared at it, the memory of the chase fresh in his mind. The initials weren't just a clue; they were a threat. Whoever had written that letter years ago still had power, still had reach. And now they knew James was close enough to be dangerous.

Elena arrived not long after. She didn't knock; Mae must have sent her up. Her hair was damp from the misty evening, her expression severe.

"You look like hell," she said.

"Appreciate the observation," James muttered.

"What happened?"

He told her about the sedan, the swerving, the near crash. Elena listened without interrupting, her jaw clenched tight.

"That's not a warning," she said when he finished. "That's attempted murder."

"I noticed," James said.

"Why didn't you call me immediately?"

"Because I wasn't sure I'd believe it myself until I calmed down," he said. "I'm not in the habit of sounding like a paranoid fool."

Her gaze softened slightly. "You're not paranoid. Whoever killed Charles and Margaret isn't finished. You've made yourself too visible. They think silencing you keeps the story clean."

James tapped his notebook on the desk. "This is the reason. Someone with these initials didn't just blackmail Charles; they controlled him. And now they're trying to control me."

"I've been through half the town's records this week," Elena said. "These initials don't match anyone obvious."

"Maybe they weren't meant to," James said. "Maybe they're a mask."

She looked at him, her eyes dark and steady. "We need to be careful, Whitaker. If you're right, we're not chasing a single murderer. The lab finished with the letter. No fingerprints or other usable evidence. I brought it because I knew you'd want to reread it—hoping it would give you some idea of who's behind the initials."

Near midnight, James went to the window. Below, Main Street was deserted, the lamps casting pale circles of light on the wet pavement. He scanned the shadows, half expecting to see the sedan waiting at the corner. But the street was empty.

He turned back to the desk, closing the notebook. He didn't need more pages that night. What he needed was resolve.

Margaret Redmond had been silenced. Charles Redmond had been ruined and killed. Evan Carlisle had been framed. And James himself had nearly been forced off the road.

The message was clear.

Chapter 7 – Betrayals Revealed

Ashwood was a town divided against itself. Margaret Redmond's drowning had rattled everyone, not just because she was wealthy and well known, but because her death came so soon after Charles's. A pattern had formed, one nobody wanted to acknowledge aloud.

In Mae's Café, James Whitaker sat sleepless in his room, haunted by headlights bearing down on him and the lurch of his car toward the ravine. He listened to fragments of conversation drifting up from the tables below.

"First Charles, now Margaret..."

"They say Evan Carlisle's behind bars. So how...?"

"Maybe there's more than one."

James sat at his desk, the notebook open, his pen tapping against the paper. He had listed names across the page, each one connected to Charles Redmond in some poisonous way. And there, written twice in bold letters, was the one name that stood out today: Daniel Harper, Hannah's fiancé. A man who stood to gain everything from Charles's death.

James arranged to meet Daniel at the Ashwood Athletic Club. It occupied a brick building on the edge of downtown, where businessmen liked to show off their racquetball skills and pretend sweat equaled power. The lounge smelled of leather polish and citrus cleaner, a place designed to make small men feel important.

Daniel Harper was waiting at a corner table, a glass of tonic water sweating on the surface before him. He wore a gray suit that fit too perfectly, his tie loosened as if to suggest he wasn't trying too hard. But the tightness in his shoulders betrayed him.

"Whitaker," he greeted, his voice smooth but guarded. "To what do I owe this unexpected visit?"

"Curiosity," James said, sliding into the chair opposite. He set his notebook down with deliberate care. "I like to know where people stood with Charles Redmond. Or what you stood to gain from his death."

Daniel's jaw flexed. "Charles and I had our differences."

"That's one way of putting it. Another is that he disapproved of your engagement and threatened to pull investment from your expansion project. Without his backing, the inn you planned with Hannah would never leave the drawing board."

Daniel's lips thinned. "That's old history. Charles was stubborn. But he's gone now, and Hannah and I—"

"Exactly," James cut in. "He's gone, and you inherit stability. Margaret's gone too. Funny timing, don't you think?"

Daniel leaned forward, eyes narrowing. "Are you accusing me?"

"I'm asking if you had something to gain," James said evenly. "From Charles's death. From Margaret's. With Charles gone, his estate passes to Margaret, who's now dead as well. Hannah inherits everything. Suddenly, your plans are safe."

Daniel's hand tightened around the glass, the ice clinking. "I loved Hannah long before Charles's money mattered. Don't you dare suggest otherwise."

"Love doesn't erase motive," James replied, jotting a note in the margin.

Daniel's composure cracked. He slapped his palm against the table, the sound echoing through the lounge. A pair of older men at the bar glanced over, whispering. Daniel noticed them and forced himself to lower his voice. "You don't know what you're talking about, Whitaker. You're chasing shadows, and if you're not careful, you'll drag Hannah's name through the mud with your wild theories."

James closed his notebook slowly. "The truth has a way of surfacing, whether I dig for it or not."

Daniel stood abruptly, his chair scraping across the floor. "Stay out of my affairs." He left without a backward glance, shoulders rigid, the tonic water untouched on the table.

Later that day, James walked into the police station, notebook tucked under his arm. Elena Marquez sat at her desk, eyes shadowed from too many sleepless nights. Papers and files cluttered every surface.

"I spoke with Daniel Harper," James began.

Elena didn't look up. "Let me guess. You think he's guilty too."

"He's hiding something," James said. "Charles's death cleared the way for his future with Hannah. Margaret's death ensured the inheritance would go to Hannah. He won't admit it, but he had motive, opportunity—"

Elena set her pen down with a sharp click. "Do you realize how you sound? Every time someone looks suspicious, you pounce. You find connections no one else sees, as if you're shaping the narrative yourself."

James frowned. "Are you suggesting I'm making this up?"

"I'm suggesting," Elena said coolly, "that you're everywhere you shouldn't be. You were at the estate the night Charles died. You found footprints. You found the blackmail letter. And now, conveniently, you're the one pointing at Daniel."

James stiffened. "If you think I killed Charles Redmond, say it outright."

Elena leaned back in her chair, folding her arms. "If you were anyone else, I'd have you in an interrogation room already. But you're Whitaker. People talk to you. They trust you. That makes you either the best ally I've got or the most dangerous liar in this town."

Anger flared in James's chest. "I want the truth, Detective. If you think I killed Charles Redmond and then Margaret Redmond, arrest me. Otherwise, stop wasting time questioning the only person in this town who isn't afraid to dig."

They stared at each other across the cluttered desk, the hum of the station filling the silence. Finally, Elena looked away, rubbing her temples. "You're reckless," she muttered. "But maybe that's what this case needs. Just don't expect me to trust you blindly."

James left the station with his pulse still hammering. Elena's suspicion stung more than he wanted to admit. But beneath his anger was something sharper: fear. If even Elena was questioning him, how long before the town did too?

That evening, James returned to Mae's Café. Downstairs was dark, chairs stacked on tables, the smell of coffee still clinging to the air. He climbed the narrow stairs to his room, exhausted but restless, and unlocked the door.

The door opened with its usual creak, but something inside felt wrong. The window over the alley was open, curtains fluttering. His notebook lay on the floor, pages scattered.

James stepped inside cautiously. His desk chair was tipped askew. Papers lay strewn across the room. The bottom drawer was open, and half its contents were spilled onto the floor.

His heart lurched. He crossed the room, kneeling to gather the scattered notes. His careful outlines, his pages of questions, his sketches of Charles's connections had all been rifled through, and some were missing. He reached for the folder where he had hidden the blackmail letter. Empty.

James swore under his breath. Whoever had broken in hadn't wanted money. His watch, wallet, and typewriter sat untouched. The intruder had come for one thing: his investigation notes.

He crouched by the desk, sifting through what remained. His pulse hammered as the whole picture sank in. The intruder hadn't taken valuables. They hadn't even disturbed his clothes or Mae's stack of neatly folded linens.

James ran a hand through his hair. That letter had been the strongest evidence yet that Charles Redmond hadn't acted alone. Someone had leaned on him, someone powerful enough to demand obedience. Now the letter was gone, erased from his grasp as if it had never existed.

He rose slowly, scanning the room. The window over the alley was unlatched, the curtains trembling in the cool night breeze. Mud streaked the sill, and on the floor just inside lay a faint smear where a boot had slid across the boards. A noise outside made James freeze.

He darted to the window, peering down into the alley. Shadows stretched long between the buildings, broken by the faint glow of a distant streetlamp. For a heartbeat, the space looked empty.

Then—movement. A figure sprinting toward the corner, coat flaring with each stride.

James didn't hesitate. He vaulted down the back stairs two at a time, hitting the ground running. His shoes slapped against the cobblestones as he chased the shadow through the narrow lane.

"Hey!" he shouted, his voice echoing.

The figure didn't slow. James caught only glimpses—broad shoulders, a dark hat pulled low—but as the runner turned sharply, something glinted in the light.

Metal. A clipped badge flashing at the belt.

James's breath caught. A police officer.

He pushed harder, lungs burning, but the intruder had the advantage. They darted into a side passage, vaulted a low fence, and disappeared into the dark beyond. By the time James scrambled after them, the alley was empty save for rustling leaves and the pounding of his own heartbeat.

He stood there, chest heaving, the truth pressing down like a lead weight.

The break-in hadn't been random. It hadn't been the work of a desperate townsman or even one of Charles's many enemies. Someone inside law enforcement had just stolen the most crucial piece of evidence in the case.

James walked back to the café in silence, each step heavier than the last. Mae met him at the door, her face pale.

"I heard shouting," she whispered. "James, what happened?"

He shook his head. "Someone broke in. Took my notes. Took the letter."

Mae's hand flew to her mouth. "Oh, Lord."

"They had a badge, Mae." His voice was low and steady despite the storm inside him. "Someone in the police force is trying to bury this."

Her eyes widened. "You have to tell Elena."

James hesitated. He pictured Elena's stern gaze, her warning words earlier that day. If he told her about the badge, would she believe him? Or would she decide he was spinning another story to deflect suspicion?

"I'll handle it," he said at last. "For now, this stays between us."

Mae frowned but didn't argue. She touched his arm briefly, then turned back into the kitchen, muttering prayers under her breath.

Alone again in his room, James gathered the few pages that remained. Most of his outlines were gone, torn clean from the notebook. The blackmail letter was, of course, missing, but oddly, the intruder had left behind one crucial page: his list of names scrawled beneath the heading Who profits here?

It felt deliberate, almost mocking. As if to say, Keep guessing, Whitaker. You'll never find me.

He sat heavily in the chair, staring at the stripped-down remnants of his work. Without the letter, he had no proof of Charles's corruption beyond rumor and resentment. Without his notes, half the threads he'd been pulling were severed.

But the chase in the alley, the flash of the badge, told him everything he needed to know. The conspiracy reached deeper than anyone suspected. And if the police were compromised, then Elena Marquez herself might not be as untouchable as she seemed.

Sleep eluded him. He spent the night piecing together what he could from memory, rewriting fragments, forcing himself to recall every word of the blackmail letter. He drew the initials again and again, each iteration angrier than the last.

By dawn, exhaustion had settled into his bones, but his resolve was sharper than ever. Someone inside Ashwood's police department was not only protecting the killer but actively sabotaging the investigation.

The question was no longer who profited from Charles's death.

It was who among the people sworn to uphold the law was willing to kill to keep their secrets hidden.

The following morning, James descended into Mae's café. She gave him a searching look as she poured his coffee, but neither spoke of the night before. Around them, townsfolk murmured over their breakfasts. Words like curse and cover-up floated through the air.

James sipped his coffee, mind racing. He couldn't tell Elena. Not until he knew whether she was the one he was chasing down those back alleys—or whether she was the only ally he had left.

But one thing was clear. The murders weren't about a single man's fortune anymore. They were about power. The kind that reaches into files, plucks out the truth, and leaves nothing but ashes.

Chapter 8 – The False Resolution

The day after the break-in, Ashwood carried the tension of a storm that never broke. Conversations cut short when James Whitaker entered a room. Old friends eyed him with suspicion, muttering behind half-raised coffee cups. He had felt like an outsider since returning, but now the distance was sharper, as though everyone sensed the gravity of what he was carrying.

James sat upstairs in his room above Mae's Café, his desk once again cluttered with scraps of notes he'd spent the night rewriting from memory. The blackmail letter was gone, but he had scrawled out every phrase he could recall. *Your debts are no longer yours... Blackmail is an ugly word... Failure will be costly.* He had even traced the initials at the bottom until the paper nearly tore.

A knock on the door broke his focus. Elena Marquez stepped in without waiting, her expression taut, hair pulled into a severe bun that emphasized the dark circles beneath her eyes.

"You're hard to find these days," she said.

"I didn't know you were looking for me," James replied.

"I wasn't. Mae was. She said you've barely eaten. That concerns me—not because I think you'll starve, but because starving men make poor witnesses. She said you chased someone who had broken into your office and saw a badge."

James gestured to the chair across from him. "Sit. We need to talk anyway."

Elena shut the door and lowered herself into the chair. Her posture was rigid, as if she didn't want to hear what he had to say. James told her about the night before—the break-in, the chase, and the badge.

"You are right," she said quietly. "There is corruption in this department. I can't deny it anymore."

James blinked, surprised at her candor. "That's not something I expected you to admit."

"I don't like saying it," Elena continued. "But I can't explain the missing evidence otherwise. Files don't vanish. Evidence doesn't walk away on its own. Someone inside is pulling strings. And now someone broke into your room."

James leaned forward. "You believe me, then?"

"I believe you saw what you saw," Elena said cautiously. "But I won't believe it was one of my closest colleagues until I have proof. These are men and women I've worked with for years."

"Trust blinds us faster than lies," James murmured.

Her eyes narrowed. "Don't push me, Whitaker. I'm here because, despite everything, I think you're onto something. Let's use that instead of tearing each other down."

They went through the suspects again, spreading notes across the desk: Hannah's scarf, Evan Carlisle's finances, Margaret Redmond's secrets, and Daniel Harper, Hannah's fiancé.

James tapped his pen against Daniel's name. "It's him. It has to be."

Elena raised an eyebrow. "You're certain?"

"Think about it," James insisted. "Charles hated the engagement. He threatened to ruin Daniel financially. If Charles had lived, Daniel's future with Hannah might have crumbled. Margaret's death secured the inheritance, leaving Daniel free to marry into fortune. He had motive and timing. And he's lied about his whereabouts more than once."

Elena frowned. "Circumstantial."

"Circumstantial piles up into a mountain if you're willing to climb it," James said.

She considered that, tapping her pen against the page. "So what are you proposing?"

"Expose him," James said simply. "Publicly. Somewhere he can't squirm his way out with vague denials."

Elena tilted her head. "Dangerous. If you're wrong, you humiliate Hannah and burn what little credibility you still have in this town."

"And if I'm right?" James countered. "Then we end this before more people die."

Elena was silent a long moment before nodding. "There's a town council reception tomorrow evening. Daniel will be there with Hannah. Half the town will be in attendance. If you want a stage, that's it."

James exhaled, his pulse quickening. Tomorrow, then. Tomorrow he would finally prove himself right.

The reception was held in town hall, a building that smelled faintly of polished wood and old paper. Chandeliers flickered overhead, casting uneven light on a crowd dressed in their Sunday best. The air buzzed with chatter, though beneath the cheer lurked unease. Ashwood had buried two of its wealthiest citizens in less than a fortnight, and now the survivors gathered to drink wine and pretend nothing was broken.

James stood near the back, notebook tucked discreetly into his jacket pocket. Elena moved through the crowd like a shadow, greeting townsfolk with professional calm while keeping her eyes on him.

Daniel arrived on Hannah's arm, looking every bit the polished fiancé. His suit was immaculate, his smile charming. Hannah, pale but smiling bravely, clung to him as if to prove—to the town and maybe herself—that everything was fine.

James's stomach tightened. He had once promised Hannah he would protect her. Exposing Daniel tonight would break her heart, but perhaps it would save her future. He waited until speeches had been made, until the mayor raised a toast to Ashwood's resilience. Glasses clinked. Murmurs filled the hall.

James stepped forward, clearing his throat. "I have something to say."

Dozens of heads turned. Daniel's smile froze. Elena stiffened across the room, eyes sharp with warning.

James lifted his voice. "We've all lost too much these past weeks. Charles Redmond. Margaret Redmond. And though we've been told Evan Carlisle is to blame, the truth is different. The truth is standing right here among us."

Gasps rippled through the crowd. Daniel's face drained of color. Hannah clutched his arm.

James drew in a breath. "Daniel Harper had both motive and opportunity. Charles despised his engagement to Hannah and threatened to end his financial support. With Charles gone, Daniel's path cleared. With Margaret gone, Hannah inherits everything—and Daniel inherits her. Ladies and gentlemen, you've been deceived."

Daniel staggered. His hand went to his chest. A glass slipped from his fingers, shattering against the floor.

"Daniel?" Hannah gasped, grabbing his arm.

Daniel's lips moved soundlessly. He convulsed, collapsing to the polished wood floor. The crowd screamed, the room erupting in chaos.

Elena pushed through, kneeling beside him, barking orders for space and silence. James stood frozen, notebook half-drawn, his accusation still hanging unfinished in the air.

Daniel's body jerked once, twice, then stilled. His eyes stared blankly at the chandelier above.

James's blood ran cold. He had been ready to expose Daniel as the murderer—and now Daniel was dead.

The reception hall dissolved into chaos. Shrieks rang out, chairs scraped, glasses tipped and shattered as guests surged toward the exits. James stood in the eye of the storm, frozen, his unfinished accusation echoing in his head. He had been so certain, so sure of Daniel's guilt—and now the man lay lifeless at his feet.

Elena crouched over Daniel's body, fingers pressed against his neck, then his wrist. Her face was grim when she looked up. "He's gone."

Hannah sobbed beside her fiancé's body, clutching his limp hand. "No, no, it can't be. Daniel!" Her wails cut through the din, raw and jagged—the sound of a future shattering.

James forced himself to kneel, his voice low. "What happened? Heart attack?"

Elena's eyes flashed. "Don't be naïve. His lips are discolored. It was poison."

James's stomach dropped. Poison. He looked at the overturned glass near Daniel's outstretched hand, liquid spreading across the floorboards.

"He drank that after I started speaking," James said. His mouth felt dry. "The drink wasn't meant for him."

Elena stiffened. "What are you saying?"

James's gaze locked on the shattered glass. "I was the one about to expose him. If he hadn't drunk from that glass, I would've. The poison was meant for me."

Elena rose sharply, turning to face him. Her voice was low but dangerous. "So not only did you nearly humiliate an innocent man in front of the entire town, but you also managed to get him killed in the process?"

"I didn't pour the drink," James snapped back. "Someone wanted me silenced. Daniel just drank from the wrong glass."

Her expression hardened. "You're reckless, Whitaker. Reckless and arrogant. You think you're the only one who sees the truth—and now a man is dead because of it."

"Daniel was hiding something," James insisted. "I may have been wrong about the murder, but he wasn't innocent. He knew more than he let on."

Hannah lifted her tear-streaked face. "Stop it. Stop it, both of you! He's dead, and you're still arguing about guilt. My Daniel is gone!" Her voice broke on the last word, and she collapsed against the mayor's wife, who guided her gently away.

Elena's voice softened slightly, but her words cut no less deep. "I warned you about chasing leads without proof. Tonight you made yourself the center of the stage, and someone took advantage of it."

James lowered his gaze. Shame warred with fury inside him. He wanted to argue, to shout, to insist he was right about the bigger picture. But the sight of Daniel's still body silenced him.

The crowd was eventually herded out under Elena's orders, the hall emptied of all but police and a few shaken council members. Daniel's body was carried away, Hannah trailing after in shock. James remained near the back wall, his notebook still clutched in his hand, pages trembling.

Elena approached him at last, arms folded. "I should bring you in. You interfered in an active investigation, disrupted a public event, and now a man is dead."

James looked up. "But you won't."

Her eyes narrowed. "Don't tempt me."

"Because you know I'm right about one thing," James pressed. "That poison wasn't meant for Daniel. It was meant for me. Someone wanted me silenced before I said too much. That means I'm close. Whoever killed Charles and Margaret doesn't just want to hide—they want me gone. This is the second attempt on my life"

"Or maybe," Elena said slowly, "they want us both chasing shadows until we destroy ourselves."

Later, after the hall had emptied and the night air pressed cool against the cobblestones, James walked alone down Main Street. His thoughts churned with guilt and determination. He had accused Daniel Harper of murder, only to watch the man collapse before his eyes. But beneath the shame was a sharper realization: someone had used the moment to try and kill him.

He replayed it in his mind—the glass in Daniel's hand, the timing, the way Elena's eyes had snapped to his when she recognized what was happening. If Daniel hadn't taken that drink, he would be the one lying in the morgue right now.

Back in his room above Mae's, James sat heavily at the desk. The window rattled faintly with the night wind. The notebook lay open before him, his handwriting frantic and jagged.

He wrote the words slowly, deliberately: *The killer is always one step ahead.*

He leaned back, rubbing his temples. Who was it? The person with initials in the blackmail letter? The shadow in the sedan that had tried to run him off the road? The intruder with the badge who had rifled through his room? Each clue twisted into another knot, and every time James thought he had grasped the truth, it slipped through his fingers. Tonight's attempt on his life made one thing clear: the killer wasn't afraid of collateral damage. Daniel's death was proof of that.

Elena came the next morning, her knock sharp before she entered. She looked tired, her face pale in the morning light.

"You're still alive," she said.

"Barely," James replied.

She closed the door and leaned against it. "The toxicology came back quicker than expected. Cyanide. Slipped into the drink at some point during the evening."

James's stomach turned. "Cyanide. That's not opportunistic. That's planned."

Elena nodded grimly. "Which means someone brought it, knowing there would be a moment to use it. They waited for you to stand up, for you to draw attention. They wanted to turn your grand reveal into your funeral."

James gave a hollow laugh. "Instead, Daniel took the wrong sip."

Elena's eyes bored into his. "Don't flatter yourself. You're not the center of this. Maybe you were a target. Maybe you weren't. Maybe Daniel was always meant to die."

"Do you believe that?" James asked.

She hesitated, then shook her head. "No. The timing was too exact. You made yourself a lightning rod, Whitaker. The killer tried to strike. They just missed."

For the rest of the morning they argued over possibilities, combing through notes and witness statements. Elena clung to procedure, to tangible evidence, while James leaned on instinct and pattern. But every path ultimately led to confusion.

At last Elena snapped her notebook shut. "You've been wrong before. Don't make me regret working with you now."

James met her gaze. "I was wrong about Daniel being the murderer. But I wasn't wrong that someone is orchestrating this—someone inside the investigation, someone with reach. And they almost got me killed last night."

Elena's voice was quiet but edged with steel. "Then we'd better figure out who it is before they try again."

That night, James stood by the window of his room, staring down at the quiet street below. Ashwood seemed calm, but he knew better. Somewhere in the darkness, someone was smiling at their success. They had turned him into a fool in front of the entire town. They had stolen his evidence, erased his leads, and nearly ended his life.

And worst of all, James realized with cold clarity, he had been chasing the wrong man from the beginning.

Daniel Harper was dead.

And the true killer was still free.

Chapter 9 – Pieces That Don't Fit

Ashwood moved like a town in mourning. Every window James passed seemed to watch him. At Mae's Café, the regular morning crowd spoke in low tones, but their eyes slid toward him when they thought he wasn't looking. Rumor had taken hold. James Whitaker had accused Daniel Harper of murder—and Daniel had dropped dead before their eyes.

Up in his room above the café, James paced the floor, replaying the scene in his mind. Daniel standing there, smiling, glass raised—then the convulsion and the collapse. He sat at his desk, the memory pressing in. Cyanide. Not something slipped in on impulse. Someone had carried it into the room and waited for the perfect moment—the exact moment he was accusing Daniel. It had been meant for him.

Voices from below filtered up.

"That's him. The cousin who stirred things up."

"Every time he opens his mouth, someone ends up dead."

Mae appeared at his desk, setting down a fresh cup of coffee and some toast. "You're not eating again."

"Not hungry," James muttered.

She looked him over with sharp eyes softened by concern. "You can't fight shadows on an empty stomach."

"I'm not fighting shadows," he said. "I'm fighting someone who wants me out of the way."

Mae's brows rose. "You think Daniel's death was meant for you?"

"I don't think," James said, voice low. "I know."

A knock interrupted them. Elena Marquez stepped inside without waiting, her uniform crisp though fatigue lined her face.

"You humiliated me last night," she said flatly.

James straightened. "Daniel's death wasn't my doing."

"You accused him in front of half the town," Elena snapped. "And now he's dead. That's what people will remember—not the poison, not the timing. Just your accusation and his body on the floor."

James met her glare. "The poison wasn't meant for him. He drank my death."

Her eyes narrowed. "You can't prove that."

"I don't need to. The timing proves it. Whoever slipped cyanide into that glass waited until I had the floor. If Daniel hadn't lifted it, I would have."

Elena crossed her arms, her posture as sharp as her tone. "Or maybe Daniel was the target all along, and you're arrogant enough to think the world spins around you."

Heat rose in James's chest. "You think this is arrogance? No. Daniel was about to be exposed. He might have confessed or defended himself. Either way, the killer couldn't risk it. They acted in that moment because of me. I was the intended victim."

Finally she said, "Even if you are right, you've made things harder. The town doesn't trust this investigation. Now they don't trust me. And frankly, I'm not sure I trust you."

The accusation struck harder than James expected. His jaw clenched. "If you think I killed them, arrest me. Otherwise, stop treating me like the villain when I'm the only one chasing the truth."

Elena's voice dropped to a knife's edge. "You're reckless. And reckless men get people killed." She turned on her heel and left, the door snapping shut behind her.

James collapsed into the chair, anger and doubt twisting inside him. Elena wasn't wrong. His pursuit of Daniel had ended in disaster. He had humiliated Hannah, destroyed what little trust he had built in Ashwood, and achieved nothing except another corpse.

That night, while rain pattered steadily against the window, James spread his notes across the desk. He went over what the blackmail letter had said—and the initials. He couldn't match them to anyone in town. He studied them again and again. Then, suddenly, they made sense.

James whispered the name aloud, as if afraid the walls might overhear.

"Elena."

He sat back in his chair, staring at the initials scrawled across the bottom of the letter he had painstakingly reconstructed. The lamp on his desk buzzed faintly, its light throwing long shadows across the cramped room. He whispered the name again, barely audible, as if speaking it too loudly might summon something terrible.

"Elena."

The name sat on his tongue like a bitter pill. He stared at the initials he had written so many times. E.M. He forced himself not to look away. He wanted to believe fatigue had warped his judgment—but the letters didn't change. They remained what they were: a signature without a name that pointed in a direction he did not want.

It couldn't be true. He wanted it not to be true. Elena Marquez was the detective who had stepped into the investigation with precision and authority, the one who had kept it from collapsing under gossip and fear. But the pieces he had been juggling for days suddenly began to fall into place, one after another, like tumblers in a lock.

Evidence appearing too conveniently. Hannah's scarf planted to frame her. Evan Carlisle's finances damning but poorly timed. Daniel's evasiveness amplified until it drew suspicion his way. Each clue had led James further from the truth—and each one had passed through Elena's hands.

He thought of the first hour at the estate, the way Elena had directed the officers. She had told them what to touch, what to send to the lab, what she would retain. He had admired her certainty. Now he replayed it differently—and found the same movements could have been planned.

James stood and began pacing, pulling at threads of memory. The night Charles was found, Elena had taken charge swiftly—too swiftly—as though she had been expecting it. The scarf had been discovered on her watch. Her team had flagged the ledger entries pointing to Evan. And at the reception, when he had stood ready to accuse Daniel, she had been there, watching, guiding.

He replayed the room in his mind, reconstructing positions. He saw Elena refuse a drink with a brief shake of her head. The waiter moved on—toward Daniel. Had she stepped closer during the toasts? He hadn't noticed. Was that drink really meant for Daniel—or for him?

He picked up his phone, typed a message to Hannah, then deleted it. She had suffered enough. He had no right to pull her deeper into this.

Elena had access to every piece of evidence, authority to shift timelines, and the power to shape witness accounts. If she wanted to weave a web of half-truths around the deaths, she had both the means and the opportunity.

But motive?

At the Redmond estate, she had insisted the scarf be catalogued quickly. At Evan's office, she had highlighted the shell companies. At the reception, she had been perfectly placed.

The pattern was subtle, almost invisible—unless one stepped back. Now James could see it clearly. She shaped the story like a novelist guiding her characters.

He remembered her words: You always seem to find leads no one else does. At the time, he had bristled. Now it sounded different. Had she been warning him—or mocking him?

James dropped into the chair, burying his face in his hands. A bitter laugh escaped him. If Elena was behind this, she had used him brilliantly. He had chased her leads, accused her suspects, and lost credibility—while she remained above suspicion.

He thought of the car that had nearly forced him off the road. The driver had been hidden—but Elena would have known where he was going. She understood his instincts better than anyone.

And the break-in. The flash of a badge. He had assumed it could have been anyone. But what if it wasn't? What if she had taken the letter herself—the one piece of evidence that pointed directly at her?

He stood again, pacing. He didn't want to believe it. He remembered her sharp wit, her discipline, the moments where she seemed almost human beneath the badge. He had trusted her.

If Elena had killed Charles—why? Revenge? Power? Fear? The letter suggested more than hatred. It suggested partnership.

James returned to his desk and organized his notes, building his case carefully. Then he made a copy. One set went into his briefcase. The other he sealed in an envelope. Across the front he wrote: To be opened if I go missing.

The next morning it dawned gray and wet. He showered, shaved, and dressed, then descended into Mae's café, the weight of his realization pressing on him. He handed her the envelope.

"Put this somewhere safe," he said quietly. "If I don't come back for it, send it to the state police—not to anyone here."

Mae studied him. "You look like you've seen a ghost."

"Maybe I have," James murmured.

"Who?"

He shook his head. "Better you don't know. Not yet."

He sipped his coffee and forced himself to eat. Outside, Elena's patrol car rolled slowly past. She didn't look up—but James felt her presence all the same.

The initials burned in his mind.

E.M.

The truth he had been chasing was suddenly too close—too dangerous. And now James Whitaker carried a secret heavier than any he had ever uncovered.

The woman leading the investigation was the killer he had been hunting all along.

Elena.

Chapter 10 – Trap of Truth

James had slept no more than an hour before the knock came. It was brisk, official, and accompanied by Elena's voice calling his name. He shoved his notes into a drawer, wiped his face with his palms, and opened the door to find her standing there with her arms crossed.

"You look worse than usual," she said, her tone clipped. "We need to go to the station and review Daniel's toxicology in more detail."

James studied her carefully. Her uniform was pressed, her hair neat, but there was a tightness around her eyes now that he couldn't unsee. It might have been fatigue. It might have been something else entirely.

He didn't need to decide what she was capable of anymore. What he needed was proof that would hold in the light. "Fine," he said, forcing a yawn. "Let me get my notebook."

As he reached for the satchel, he slipped a folded scrap of paper inside, positioning it so that when he opened the notebook later, it would fall naturally. The note was bait—nothing more than a fabricated witness near the textile mill, a man who claimed to have seen someone leaving the Whitaker estate on the night of Charles' murder. It didn't need to be convincing. It only needed to be followed.

"I'll drive," Elena said.

James nodded, locking the door behind him. The morning air was damp and gray, the kind that settled into clothing and stayed there. They rode to the station in silence, the hum of the engine filling the space between them. James watched her hands on the wheel, steady and controlled, as if nothing in the world could shake her.

Inside the station, Elena moved with her usual authority, directing officers, absorbing updates, never hesitating. The room bent subtly around her presence, people adjusting their movements without realizing they were doing it. James had once admired that.

Now he studied it.

They settled into a cramped conference room, the fluorescent lights buzzing faintly overhead. Elena spread the toxicology report across the table, running her finger down the columns as she spoke.

"Cyanide," she said. "Introduced at the last moment. Which means whoever did it was close to the drink and knew when to act."

"Or," James said, keeping his tone even, "they knew when everyone would be watching me."

Her gaze flicked up briefly. "You're still convinced it was your glass?"

"Yes."

She held his eyes for a moment longer than necessary, then leaned back slightly. "Then we're looking for someone inside the investigation."

The answer came too easily, too cleanly. James nodded as if persuaded and opened his notebook. The folded scrap slipped free, landing faceup on the table between them.

Elena's eyes dropped to it for less than a second before returning to the report, but James caught the subtle tightening of her fingers against the paper in front of her. It was a small reaction, almost nothing at all, yet it was enough.

He said nothing.

When the meeting ended, James stepped out into the damp morning and walked a short distance down Main Street before stopping beneath an awning. He waited, watching the station doors through the misting drizzle.

A short time later, Elena emerged with purpose in her stride, her phone already at her ear. She didn't hesitate or pause to question. She moved as if the next step had already been decided.

The following morning, Mae mentioned casually while wiping down the counter, "Police were out by the old textile mill," she said. "Some young officer chasing a lead."

James didn't react outwardly, but something inside him settled. Elena hadn't questioned the note.

She had acted on it. That wasn't instinct. That was control.

He spent the afternoon preparing the second test, making it tighter and more deliberate. This time, the note suggested that Margaret Redmond had left a second will, hidden in a lockbox at her sister's house outside town.

The next morning, Elena requested his notebook again.

"Cross-reference," she said.

James handed it over without hesitation. The paper slipped free just as before. She glanced at it briefly, slid it back into place, and returned the notebook without comment when she was through with it.

By evening, Denise called, her voice sharp with anger. "Do you know why the police were at my aunt's house today? They went through everything."

James closed his eyes. The second test had worked just as cleanly as the first.

Elena didn't verify information. She deployed it.

Now he needed to prove it somewhere it couldn't be ignored.

The mayor's town meeting gave him the opportunity. The town hall smelled of floor polish and nervous perfume. Rows of folding chairs faced the dais, and the low murmur of conversation carried the uneasy rhythm of a town trying to convince itself things were under control. James stood near the back, his satchel pressed against his side, the final note folded small inside.

Mae brushed his arm as she passed. "You don't have to be the loudest voice," she said softly.

"I won't be. Just the right one," he replied.

Elena entered last, composed as ever, her presence settling the room in a way no speech ever could. She took her place at the front, calm and precise, and began speaking with the steady cadence the town had come to trust.

When she began speaking, he moved.

As a volunteer passed down the aisle checking exits, James stepped forward just enough to brush shoulders with him. "Sorry," he murmured, letting the folded scrap slip from his fingers. It dropped against the man's shoe and caught there. A few steps later, the volunteer noticed it, bent, and picked it up without breaking stride, glancing at it briefly before tucking it into his vest.

The final note was simple and precise: Vestry closet. Behind hymnals. Bloodied glove. Left hand.

James stepped back into place and waited.

Minutes passed. Elena continued speaking, her tone measured, controlled.

Then Elena glanced offstage. An officer moved. Another followed. No hesitation. No question. Just action.

The last of James's doubts settled into something solid.

When the side door opened and a message was delivered, the shift in Elena's expression was subtle, but it was there. A flicker. Gone almost instantly.

"We will pause briefly," she said into the microphone. "Please remain seated."

She stepped off the dais.

James followed.

The hallway beyond was bright and quiet, the sounds of the crowd muffled behind closed doors. He reached the doorway just as Elena issued the order.

"Check the vestry. Now."

"Bad time?" James asked, his tone casual.

She turned toward him without surprise. "Mr. Whitaker."

A brief pause, precise as a held breath.

He didn't move. "You didn't ask where the note came from," James continued, his voice steady. "You didn't ask why the first two were in my notebook, or how I got it. The first time, you ignored it. The second time, you ignored it again. A detective doesn't overlook something like that unless they already know what they're going to do with it."

Her expression remained composed, but her eyes sharpened slightly. "I don't ignore potential evidence," she said.

"Or you don't question it," James replied.

Footsteps thundered down the hall as the officers returned, moving fast, energized.

"Detective," the sergeant said, holding up a sealed evidence bag. Inside was a dark-stained glove. "Exactly where the tip said."

James didn't look at it. He watched Elena.

She took the bag, her grip tightening for a fraction of a second before settling into something practiced and controlled.

"There it is," James said quietly.

She said nothing.

"You followed the first note to the mill," he continued. "You sent officers to Denise's aunt's house on the second. And now this. Every lead I planted, you turned into action without question."

The words hung in the air.

The sergeant shifted uneasily, glancing between them.

Elena dismissed him with a warning to keep all of this quiet.

Her expression remained composed, but something behind it had changed—just enough to be seen if you were looking for it.

Elena's voice, when it came, was calm. "You think very highly of your own importance."

"No," James replied evenly. "I think very clearly about your behavior."

He stepped closer, reached into his satchel and placed the reconstructed letter on the table between them.

"E.M."

Her eyes flicked down to it, then back to him.

"Initials prove nothing," she said.

"Patterns do."

Silence stretched, thin and taut.

The murmur of the crowd pressed faintly through the walls as Elena stepped closer, closing the space between them. Up close, the control in her expression felt less like confidence and more like something carefully maintained.

"You've built a theory," she said.

"I've built a pattern," he replied.

"And patterns can be misleading."

"Only when they're accidental."

For a moment, neither moved.

Then, for the first time, something shifted. It wasn't dramatic. It was smaller than that. A softening at the edge of her voice, the faintest release of the control she had held so tightly.

"You're closer than you should be," she said.

James held her gaze. "That's because you let me get there."

A faint smile touched her lips, almost imperceptible, but unmistakably real.

"You should have left it alone, James."

Chapter 11 – The Shattering Reveal

The hum of voices in the hall rolled like distant thunder as Elena and James reentered from the side room. The mayor smiled stiffly and gestured toward the lectern again, filling the pause with empty words about community strength. Elena strode back to her place, calm restored, her dark jacket smooth, her badge catching the light. James slipped into a chair halfway down the aisle, his pulse hammering so loudly it seemed impossible the crowd did not hear it.

Mae caught his eye from across the room. She sat rigid, her hands folded tight in her lap, the question in her gaze simple and unspoken: Are you going to do it now? James gave the smallest nod. Near the back wall, two unfamiliar men stood apart from the crowd, watching more than listening, their attention fixed not on the mayor but on the room itself. James noted them briefly, then let his focus return to the front. The moment had arrived, and there would be no stepping back from it.

Elena adjusted the microphone, her voice crisp and controlled. "Ladies and gentlemen, as I stated earlier, we have retrieved additional evidence this evening. A glove was found that may connect to the Redmond case. Our lab will analyze the sample. I ask for your patience as we continue to pursue justice." A murmur rippled through the crowd, some nodding in reassurance while others frowned, their confidence beginning to fray.

James rose before she could continue. "Patience is not what Ashwood needs," he said, his voice carrying to the back rows. "What

Ashwood needs is the truth." Dozens of heads turned, and the mayor blinked, uncertain, looking from James to Elena. Elena did not turn. She stood at the lectern, one hand gripping the wood, the other resting lightly on her notes, but James saw her knuckles whiten.

"I have been watching this investigation from the inside," James continued, taking slow, deliberate steps toward the front. "And what I've seen isn't a search for truth. It's a pattern."

The mayor half-rose in protest, but Elena's voice cut across him, cool and precise. "He is not an officer. He has no authority."

"No," James replied, "but I have eyes. And I've been paying attention." The room leaned toward him—curious, uneasy, waiting—as he stopped a few feet from the dais.

"Hannah's scarf was planted. Evan Carlisle was convenient—financially guilty, perhaps, but not a killer. Margaret Redmond was silenced. And Daniel Harper..." He paused, steadying himself. "Daniel died drinking poison meant for me." Gasps broke across the hall, and James lifted his gaze, sweeping the room as unease deepened into something closer to fear.

"Every time suspicion settled, evidence appeared—clean, timely, convenient. Not discovered, but placed. You see the pattern? Someone wasn't following the trail. They were laying it." A voice from the back called out, "By who?" and the question seemed to settle over the crowd like a weight.

James turned toward the lectern. "By the person controlling the investigation. The person you trusted to find the truth. Detective Elena Marquez."

The room erupted—gasps, cries, shouted denials. Chairs scraped as people half-rose or shrank back. Mae covered her mouth with both hands, and the mayor stammered in disbelief. Elena lifted a hand, and silence fell, not because she demanded it, but because people still believed she deserved it.

"Mr. Whitaker is grieving," she said calmly. "He has become obsessed. He twists coincidence into conspiracy." Her composure held, but the edge beneath it had sharpened.

James did not flinch. "Then explain this," he said. "Every false lead I created became real. The mill. The house. The vestry tonight. You didn't question them. Two notes falling out of my notebook and you read them, but didn't acknowledge them. Didn't ask how I got them or why I hadn't brought them to you. You just —you acted on them. You knew they were false leads because you hadn't planted them yourself." A murmur spread again, sharper now, voices rising in uncertain agreement.

"I saw the police at the mill," someone said. "And my sister's house," another added, the words carrying farther than intended. Doubt began to ripple where certainty had once been.

Elena's eyes narrowed slightly. "Fabrications," she said. "A man playing games."

James reached into his satchel and lifted the reconstructed letter. "Charles Redmond received this. A blackmail letter—debts, control, payment. And it's signed with two initials." He held it higher, letting the silence gather. "E.M."

Shock moved through the crowd like a slow wave. Elena leaned toward the microphone, her voice measured and precise. "A reconstruction. Not an original. No chain of custody. No evidentiary value."

"Maybe not in court," James said, stepping closer, "but patterns don't need permission to be true. You controlled the scenes. You directed the evidence."

A flicker crossed Elena's face, small but unmistakable, and James pressed forward.

"Charles Redmond abandoned your mother," he said. "Left her with nothing while he built his reputation here. You grew up watching this town praise him. You didn't forget. You waited. And when you had power, you used it."

Elena's composure shifted—not broken, but strained. "You're building a story," she said.

"I'm describing one. I'm a journalist. I check things out thoroughly before I make a statement or write a paper." James replied.

Her voice sharpened. "Charles Redmond destroyed lives and called it business. This town watched him do it and said nothing." The words landed harder than any confession, and a few people in the crowd looked down, unwilling to meet one another's eyes.

"You don't get to decide who lives and dies," James said.

"And you think justice always comes through a courtroom?" Elena shot back. "You think the law catches everything?" Her voice had changed now, stripped of polish, carrying something raw beneath it. "He wasn't a victim. He was a consequence."

The room recoiled. James held her gaze. "And Margaret?" he asked.

Elena's jaw tightened.

"She knew," James continued. "She lived with his secrets long enough to recognize yours."

A flicker again—this time unmistakable.

"And Daniel?" James pressed. "Wrong place. Wrong moment. He drank what was meant for me." The crowd broke into overlapping voices, fear and outrage rising together.

"My mother was the Redmond's housekeeper. He mistreated her, took advantage of her. Threatened her if she said anything. Got her pregnant and then threw her out with no family and no where to go.. She had to find menial work just to keep alive and take care of me. We lived on the upper floor of an old smelly fish house, with little heat and no electricity. He thought because he was part of the rich and elite, he had the right to treat people as he wished"

Elena slammed her hand against the lectern, the crack silencing the room. "You think you understand any of this?" she said, her voice raw now. "You think you know what it is to grow up erased? To watch your mother break while the man responsible is celebrated?"

"That's not justice," James said.

"No," she replied. "It isn't. Yes, I murdered him and I am not sorry"

The admission was quiet, but it landed with devastating clarity. The room became silent as the stunned audience tried to absorb what they just heard.

She continued, "I did not kill anyone else. Even though I suspected Margaret was aware of the truth, I also knew she would still keep quiet. I had no reason to hurt Daniel. And, I didn't try to kill you.

"Maybe not," James said, "But you are still involved in blackmail and consorting to cheat the innocent people of this town.

James saw Hannah in the second row, her hands clenched in her lap, her eyes hollow with a grief that had not yet found shape. He saw Denise beside her, rigid and watchful. He thought of Daniel's body hitting the floor. Of Margaret in the tub. Of Charles slumped on the bench beneath the fog.

Movement at the back drew every eye. The two men James had noticed earlier stepped forward, flashing badges. "Detective Elena Marquez," one said firmly, "you are under arrest for the murder of Charles Redmond and the conspiracy to commit fraud.

The room erupted again, louder, more chaotic. Elena turned, her eyes locking onto James. "You called them."

"I made sure you couldn't control this one," he said.

She moved quickly, but the officer was faster, securing her weapon before she could draw it. The cuffs snapped shut, and gasps turned to cries as the reality of the moment settled over the crowd.

"You don't understand what he did!" Elena shouted. "What this town allowed! You'll thank me one day!"

But her words no longer carried authority. She was led from the room through a corridor of stunned faces, her badge catching the light one last time before disappearing.

James stood still, the noise of the room distant now, hollow and unreal. Mae reached him, gripping his arm. "You did it," she whispered.

James shook his head slowly. "No," he said. "I ended it."

He looked toward the empty lectern, the fallen microphone humming faintly, and around him the town unraveled—voices raised, truths colliding, certainty gone. He had uncovered the truth, but it tasted like ash. Because somewhere beneath the shock and betrayal, a quieter and far more dangerous thought lingered.

Elena hadn't been entirely wrong.

Chapter 12 – Ashes of the Past

The next morning, Ashwood felt like a town without a heartbeat. Streets that usually stirred with chatter and errands moved sluggishly, as if the air had thickened overnight. Shopkeepers opened their doors in silence. Curtains that once twitched at gossip stayed drawn. It was as though the whole town had been caught staring into a mirror and had not liked what it saw.

James walked the length of Main Street, his hands shoved deep into his coat pockets. The bells over Mae's Café door jingled behind him as he left with coffee in a paper cup, but the warmth did little to ease the cold inside him. Every few steps, someone looked his way—sometimes with gratitude, sometimes with fear, and sometimes with something darker he could not name. He was the man who had ripped the mask off Ashwood's detective.

He had told the truth, and yet he felt no victory.

Mae caught up with him near the square, her apron strings still tied, her eyes sharp with worry. "You shouldn't be walking alone," she said.

James sipped his coffee. "I'm fine."

"You're not," she said flatly. "And neither is this town. Half of them are calling you a hero. The other half think you've ruined us."

"Maybe they're both right," James said.

Mae sighed, falling into step beside him. "You did what had to be done. But don't expect them to thank you for it. Ashwood likes its illusions neat. You broke them wide open."

James stopped, watching a group of townsfolk hurry past with their eyes downcast. "I wonder if I should have left it alone," he murmured.

Mae turned on him sharply. "Don't you dare say that. If you had walked away, Elena would still be standing up there, pointing fingers at anyone she pleased. People would still be dying."

Later, he found Hannah on the estate grounds, her shoulders hunched beneath a shawl, her gaze fixed on the pavilion where it had all begun. She didn't hear him approach until Koby, the gardener's old dog, padded over and nudged her hand.

"James," she said softly, her voice hoarse.

He hesitated, unsure whether she wanted his presence. But she gave a faint smile, weary but real.

"You were right about everything," she said. "And I hate that you were."

James sat beside her on the cold stone bench. "I didn't want to be."

Hannah's eyes glistened. "Daniel wasn't perfect. Maybe he had reasons I'll never know. But he didn't deserve to die like that. And now the detective I thought was protecting us..." She broke off, pressing her fingers to her lips.

James placed a hand lightly on her arm. "None of us deserved this. Not you. Not Daniel. Not Ashwood."

In the afternoon, he sat at the back of the town council chamber as officials stumbled through a meeting meant to restore confidence. The mayor's voice wavered as he promised cooperation with state authorities. Council members avoided each other's eyes.

The citizens in attendance looked more like survivors of a storm than a community.

James listened, but his thoughts drifted. He thought of Elena's final words in the hall: *You should have left it alone, James.* He thought of the fury in her eyes, the pain in her voice when she spoke of her mother. It was a wound that had festered until it consumed everything.

And yet, even knowing her motive, he could not excuse what she had done. Revenge was not justice. Murder was not redemption.

That evening, Mae closed the café early. She found James sitting upstairs in his rented room, notes scattered across the desk once more.

"You should rest," she said, her tone gentle this time.

"I can't," he admitted. "Not yet. Every time I close my eyes, I see her face. The way she looked when I said her father's name. The way the town looked when the cuffs went on."

Mae sat across from him, folding her hands. "You didn't create her sins. You just revealed them."

James rubbed his temples. "That's the part I can't let go of. I've spent my life uncovering stories, writing them down for people who never knew the cost. But this one isn't just words on a page. These are lives. Ashwood will never look the same to itself again."

Mae reached across the desk, covering his hand with hers. "Maybe it shouldn't. Maybe that's the only way forward."

He looked at her, the lines of exhaustion softening in her face. "And what about me?" he asked.

She smiled faintly. "Maybe you're not meant to run off again. Maybe you're meant to stay. Help pick up the pieces. God knows we'll need someone who can still see the truth even when it hurts."

James didn't answer, but the thought stayed with him long after she had gone back downstairs.

Night fell early over Ashwood, drawing a dark shawl across the rooftops and soaking the town in a hush that felt earned. James Whitaker stood at his window above Mae's Café and watched the streetlamps punch neat circles into the drizzle. Across the way, the tailor's neon sign buzzed to life, humming like a tired insect. The day had been long. Apologies were offered with brittle smiles, statements were recorded, and reporters from the county paper knocked on doors. He should have felt finished. He didn't.

He turned from the glass and faced the small room that had learned his patterns. The scattered notes multiplied every time he swore he'd pare them down. The notebook lay open to a page he'd titled, perhaps too dramatically, *What's Left When the Story Ends*. He sat, ran his finger beneath the words, and began to answer himself out loud.

"What's left is a town with a hole where trust used to be," he said softly. "What's left is a detective in cuffs and a dozen questions still crowding the door."

He reached for the file folder at the corner of the desk that contained his reconstructed letter, the timeline grids, and the list of "moments that didn't fit" that had stubbornly insisted on a meaning no one wanted. He slid them into a clean envelope and wrote, in a steady hand, Ashwood—Phase Two. The title struck him as grimly funny. He wasn't sure whether he had just christened a case or admitted an addiction.

A light knock sounded at the door. Mae entered without waiting, balancing a tray with two mugs and a plate that smelled of cinnamon and butter. Her eyes did a quick inventory of the room. "You've been staring at the same page for half an hour," she said.

She set the tray down, pushed a mug toward him, and took the chair by the window. "Anything I can say to help?"

"You've already said it," James answered. "Eat. Sleep. Don't carry the weight alone. All the good counsel people forget to follow because it arrives in ordinary words."

She smiled without showing teeth. "You think you'll go?"

He hesitated, then shook his head. "No. I was halfway to the door at noon. By four, I wanted to run until the county was way behind me. But the longer I sat with it, the more I realized leaving would be the second betrayal. Elena taught Ashwood to doubt the badge. If I go now, I teach them to doubt the pen too."

Mae sipped her tea. "So you'll stay."

"For a while," he said.

Mae nodded once, satisfied. "Then I'll raise your rent a dollar and call it a pledge of civic duty."

He laughed, and in the wake of that laugh felt something like breath return. "Deal," he said.

She sobered. "People will choose their version of you. Some will make you a hero. Some will make you the man who threw a torch into a dry barn. Try not to believe either."

They talked a while in the unhurried way of people who have earned silence. Mae told him the school had sent a letter promising counselors for the children. James told her Denise planned to leave town for a week and breathe somewhere that didn't smell like red clay and old money. Hannah would stay, he said, because she had a house and a name and a grief that didn't travel well. When Mae rose to go, she left the plate behind and took nothing except the assurance that morning would still arrive.

After the door clicked shut, James ate half the biscuit and set the rest aside, not because he was full, but because saving something small for later felt like a sign of faith. He cleaned the desk not out of compulsion, but out of a desire to begin again without tripping over old debris. Folders went into stacks. Pens were capped and lined up like tiny sentries. A single page sat at the center of the blotter with a blank top margin waiting for a date.

Instead, he wrote in the lower left corner, where a teacher had once taught him to tuck important truths: *Elena's confession was not a key; it was a siren.* She had said enough to poison the town against its own comfort, but not enough to map every step. He owed Ashwood more than a headline and a bruise. He owed it the tedious, stubborn work that followed the fireworks—the cross-checks, the affidavits, and the question, where were you?

When he could no longer sit still, he put on his coat and went down the narrow staircase. The café was dim and tidy, with chairs upended on tables and counters wiped to a soft gleam. He let himself out the back door into the cool alley air. The rain had loosened to a mist that gave the streetlights halos. Somewhere, a freight train made the far hills hum.

He walked the long way to the square. The town had the gorgeous look of places in bad movies, beautiful and empty at the same time. In the florist's window, bouquets glowed like small lanterns. In the barbershop, the striped pole turned—slow, relentless, patriotic. He turned his collar up and let Main Street tell him its story in small, ordinary phrases: J.C. Larkin's cough as he locked up, Mrs. Vidal's cat lifting its head from the bakery doorway, the smell of wet creosote rising from the utility pole where teenagers carved initials. He looked at the post office boxes in the lobby, sturdy metal doors in neat rows. He opened his little box with the brass key Mae had put on a ribbon and found three things: a coupon for tires, a postcard from a friend who never stopped sending them even when James forgot to answer, and an envelope without a stamp, hand-delivered, addressed in tidy print: J. Whitaker.

He felt it before he understood it—the prickle along his scalp, the small vertigo that says the ground is about to tilt. He looked up and down the street, though he knew how ridiculous and how necessary that was. A couple walked arm in arm beneath a shared umbrella, their laughter soft. A police cruiser idled by the bank, its silhouette shifting behind the glass. No one crouched in a trench coat and hat. He tucked the envelope into his jacket and walked back to the café at a measured pace. In the alley, he stopped, glanced once at the stairwell window to make sure no shadow waited there, then climbed.

Upstairs, he did not open the envelope at the desk. He stood by the window because he wanted the town in his periphery when he learned what it had decided to do with him next. He slid a finger under the flap and lifted it carefully, as if the contents might sting.

There was one piece of folded paper, no letterhead, no smudge to date it. He unfolded it and saw a single line in a hand that practiced neatness the way some practice cruelty.

You uncovered Elena, but you didn't uncover me.

No signature. No initials. As if the writer had read his notes and decided to spare him the small mercy of a hint. He read it twice more, not because he hadn't understood but because repetition made it real, and then set it on the sill and looked out at the town.

His phone buzzed on the desk. A text from the state investigator—Caldwell, the man with the gray at his temples. *We'll need you tomorrow for sworn statements. 9 a.m., town hall side office. We'll keep this clean, Mr. Whitaker.* James typed back, *I'll be there,* and set the phone facedown. He trusted Caldwell about as far as a man can trust another man whose job is deciding which truths survive. It was enough for now.

He stared at the envelope again, impressed by its restraint. No flourish, no threat, nothing melodramatic. Just the line. It had the confidence of someone who believed they could send a message and continue their normal routine. "You're still out there," James said to the room. "And you know I know you are."

He cleared a corner of the desk and began assembling the binder he would carry in the morning: the letter copies, the time grids, the notes from Hannah and Denise, and the transcripts of the calls he had recorded with permission. He added a fresh pad and a second pen because he had learned that pens die during essential moments, and he refused to give fate a prop.

He turned off the lamp and let the streetlight take over the room. At the window, he pressed his palm to the glass and looked down at the door he used each morning and night. "I'm staying," he said to the empty room, because he needed to hear it said. "I'm staying, and I will do this the slow way."

He stood there until the night deepened, the last car had gone home, and the rain gave up altogether. When he finally stepped back, he slid the chair under the desk, checked the window latch—an old habit made new again—and went to the bed without undressing, because he knew sleep would be brief. But before he lay down, he picked up the single-page note one more time and held it close to his face, trying to catch a scent. It smelled faintly of cologne and paper dust. He smiled despite himself. An accomplice who leaves no traceable scent was worth his attention.

He set the note back in the sleeve and placed it on the desk where the first light would find it. Downstairs, a floorboard sighed as Mae moved through the café to check the ovens the way she always did before she let herself rest. The sound traveled up through the old building and into his bones, fixing him to the place he had chosen.

James did not sleep so much as drift, anchored by the sentence that had arrived to push him past endings and into beginnings. He hadn't won anything. He had crossed from one room to another and found the second room darker. But he knew where the light switches were, and he was less afraid of the dark.

When his eyes opened again, the night had shifted but not fled. The window showed him a town that would wake whether it wanted to or not. He rose, went to the desk, and put his hand on the folder that now held two threats and one promise.

You uncovered Elena, the note had said. *But you didn't uncover me.*

"Not yet," he said. "But I will."

PART TWO

Chapter 13 - Picking Up The Pieces

Morning came cold and bright—a light that revealed more than it comforted. Ashwood lay beneath a brittle silence, the kind that follows catastrophe. Elena Marquez's betrayal had spread far beyond the town limits. Reporters had arrived in droves, crowding the station with flashing cameras, demanding interviews from anyone who could so much as spell her name.

James Whitaker avoided them all. He walked down Main Street with his collar turned up, his thoughts heavy and unsettled. It had been three days since Elena's arrest, and still he couldn't sleep through the night. The sound of handcuffs, her voice echoing—You should have left it alone, James—haunted him like a refrain he couldn't silence.

Mae had tried to keep the café open as usual, but business was slow. People came in quietly, ordered, and left with their heads down. Ashwood's faith in law and order had crumbled overnight.

When James came down the stairs that morning, Mae looked up from the counter, her smile faint but kind. "You look like you've been up since yesterday," she said.

"Maybe the day before," James admitted. He took his usual seat near the window. "Any sign of calm returning?"

Mae shrugged. "Depends on what you call calm. The council's meeting again today—another emergency session. They say the state's sending someone new to help the department. About time."

James nodded absently, staring into his coffee. The last detective they'd sent had turned out to be a murderer. Whoever came next had a long way to climb.

Mae hesitated, then said softly, "I saw you on the news last night. They called you 'the man who brought down Ashwood's hero.'"

He grimaced. "That's one way to phrase it."

"She fooled everyone," Mae said gently. "Don't carry that weight like it's yours."

James managed a small, tired smile. "I'll try."

At noon, the town hall filled once more with council members, a few reporters, and a scattering of citizens too curious to stay home. The mayor, haggard but determined, stood at the podium and tapped the microphone.

"Ladies and gentlemen," he began, "Ashwood has been through something terrible. Detective Marquez's actions have wounded our community and shaken our faith in justice. But the state has not abandoned us. Today, I'm proud to introduce the officer who will lead our department's recovery—Detective Naomi Pierce."

Applause came, tentative but genuine. From the side door stepped a woman in her late thirties. She was tall and poised, her dark hair pulled neatly back, her expression steady without being cold. She wore a simple navy suit instead of a full uniform, and her badge gleamed against the lapel. There was none of Elena's flair for command, none of her theatrical confidence. Naomi radiated quiet authority, the kind that didn't demand obedience but invited it.

"Thank you, Mayor," she said. Her voice carried clearly—measured and calm. "I've been briefed on the Marquez investigation and the events that followed. I won't pretend this is an easy situation. Trust is fragile, and I don't expect it to be given freely. But I intend to earn it."

A murmur of approval ran through the room. Even James, standing at the back, felt something in his chest loosen.

Naomi glanced toward him. "And," she continued, "I'll be working closely with Mr. Whitaker. His insight into the case proved invaluable, and his understanding of this town may help us uncover anything we've missed."

James blinked, startled. The last detective had treated him like a nuisance. Naomi Pierce was something entirely different.

After the meeting, the crowd thinned quickly. James lingered near the exit, unsure whether to introduce himself. He didn't have to wait long. Naomi approached, a faint smile touching her lips.

"Mr. Whitaker," she said. "I've read your reports. You did remarkable work under impossible circumstances."

He hesitated. "You mean I got lucky."

Her eyes—an unreadable shade of gray-blue—held his. "Luck doesn't line up evidence and see through lies."

"Maybe not," he said, "but it can put you in the wrong place at the right time."

Naomi studied him a moment longer. "Maybe. But I prefer to believe people earn their discoveries."

He found himself returning her smile. "You might be the first detective in Ashwood to say that without an insult attached."

"Then let's hope I'm not the last," she replied.

They walked together down the courthouse steps. The afternoon wind stirred brown leaves along the curb, their brittle rustle filling the pauses between words.

Naomi glanced sideways. "You look tired."

"Probably because I am," James said. "It's hard to rest when you're wondering what you've missed."

Her brow furrowed slightly. "You mean the letter?"

He stopped. "You've heard about that?"

She nodded. "Caldwell briefed me. He said you received an anonymous note implying another conspirator was involved. I believe him."

"You do?"

"Of course," she said. "Elena couldn't have orchestrated all of this alone. Too many moving parts—logistics, accounts, coded ledgers. Someone clever enough to stay invisible."

James studied her, impressed. "You've done your homework."

Naomi's tone softened. "I don't like ghosts, Mr. Whitaker. And whoever wrote that letter isn't done haunting this town."

"Call me James," he said quietly.

She gave a slight nod. "Naomi."

The exchange lingered between them—the first step of an alliance.

Later that evening, James found Naomi waiting for him at Mae's Café. She had traded her formal jacket for a wool coat, her expression grave.

"Could we talk privately?" she asked.

Mae, ever discreet, gestured toward the stairs. "You can use his room. I'll keep the coffee hot."

They climbed the narrow staircase. In James's small apartment, Naomi moved to the window, her gaze flicking to the street below as if checking for eavesdroppers. Then she turned and set an envelope on his desk.

"This was found in Elena's belongings," she said. "Locked in the false bottom of her desk drawer. It was addressed to you."

James stared at it. His name was written in Elena's sharp, elegant hand.

"Why would she keep something like this?" he asked. "I don't know,"

Naomi said quietly. "But you should see what's inside."

James broke the seal carefully. Inside were folded sheets of thick paper covered in strange symbols, shorthand, and columns of numbers. Some were circled, others marked with slashes. It looked like a ledger, but the entries made no sense at first glance.

At the bottom, one detail caught his eye.

The same initials as before—E.M.

He looked up at Naomi, his pulse quickening. "This isn't over."

She nodded grimly. "No. It's just beginning."

Outside, a siren wailed in the distance, echoing off the dark facades of Ashwood's sleeping streets—an omen of the shadows yet to come.

The storm that had threatened all day finally broke. Rain swept across Ashwood in silver sheets, tapping the café windows with soft insistence. Upstairs, James and Naomi sat at his narrow desk, the small lamp between them illuminating the strange ledger Elena had left behind.

James traced a line down the page. "It's not just numbers," he said. "Some entries repeat in patterns, but not consistently. It's not a balance sheet."

Naomi leaned closer. "It looks like a cipher. Columns of coded names, maybe. Each line ends with a two-letter marker—sometimes the same, sometimes different." She pointed. "And that one—E.M.—appears again and again. Elena wasn't hiding this from others. She was documenting it for someone."

James exhaled slowly. "So she kept records for her partner."

"Or her controller," Naomi said. "The question is why she'd risk writing it down."

Rain drummed harder against the glass, muffling the town's distant hum. James turned another page. Some entries were marked with geometric symbols—triangles, circles, squares—in red ink. Others were crossed out in pencil. Whatever system Elena used, it had meaning buried beneath deliberate confusion.

"Look at the dates," James said. "They're sequential, but they don't align with the timeline of the murders. She started this before Charles Redmond's death."

Naomi frowned. "Then this ledger isn't about covering her crimes. It's about what led her there."

"A breadcrumb trail," he said.

They worked in silence for a while, the only sounds were the scratch of Naomi's pen and the steady hiss of rain. Occasionally, Mae's footsteps creaked below as she moved through the closed café, unaware of the quiet unraveling above her.

Finally, Naomi pushed back her chair. "There's something else you should see." She reached into her coat pocket and produced a small plastic evidence bag. Inside was a brass key, old-fashioned, with the number 9 etched into its head.

"Elena kept this in her locker," Naomi said. "No tag. No address."

James turned it over in the light. "It's not from her apartment. And it's not a safety deposit box key. It's too large."

"Maybe a storage unit?" Naomi suggested.

"Or a safe," James murmured. "Number nine… the ninth ledger entry, maybe?" He glanced down at the open page. Entry 9 was one of the few not coded. It simply read, *Deliveries confirmed. Final phase approved. E.M.'*

Naomi met his eyes. "If there was a 'final phase,' someone else had to approve it."

James felt the familiar unease stir. "Meaning whoever sent that letter is still out there."

"And watching," Naomi said quietly.

By morning, the rain had cleared, leaving the streets washed clean and shining. James hadn't slept. He and Naomi had gone over every page of the ledger twice, deciphering what little they could. It remained a riddle without a key.

He found Naomi downstairs, nursing a cup of coffee while Mae arranged pastries behind the counter, sensing the heaviness between them.

Naomi gestured for him to sit. "I made a few calls to the state forensics lab," she said. "They're sending a specialist to analyze the ink and paper. But whatever we find, I want to approach this from both sides—science and intuition."

James raised an eyebrow. "Intuition?"

"Your kind of intuition," she said. "The kind that saw what everyone else missed."

He studied her a moment, still not used to the easy respect in her tone. "Elena wouldn't have liked that comparison."

Naomi smiled faintly. "No, I suppose she wouldn't."

Her phone buzzed. She glanced down, then answered. "Pierce," she said briskly. She listened, then nodded. "Understood. I'll review them personally." She ended the call and looked at James. "The evidence team finished cataloguing Elena's personal effects. Notebooks, a few data drives—and, oddly, a jewelry box containing nothing but spare keys."

"Keys," James repeated. "Plural?"

"Eight of them, numbered one through eight," Naomi said. "The one we found last night completes a set."

"So she meant them to be found together," James said. "A sequence."

Naomi nodded. "Or a message."

He rubbed his temples. "If it's a system, each key could correspond to something—a location, a file, an account."

"That's my thinking too," she said. "And I intend to find out what they open."

James drew a slow breath. "Elena wasn't just keeping records—she was building insurance. Something to protect herself if her partner turned on her."

Naomi's expression darkened. "And now that she's in lockup, those keys may be the only thing keeping her accomplice nervous."

Later that day, Naomi brought James to the precinct's evidence room. It smelled faintly of old paper and disinfectant. A row of labeled boxes lined one wall. She retrieved one marked MARQUEZ, E. – PERSONAL EFFECTS and set it on the table.

Inside were the eight smaller keys, a stack of handwritten notes, and a sealed plastic pouch containing a flash drive. James picked up one of the keys. It matched the one from Elena's locker exactly, each engraved with a number from 1 to 8.

"Who numbered these?" he asked.

"Her, most likely," Naomi said. "No evidence tags match the numbers."

He frowned. "You mentioned notebooks?"

She opened one. The handwriting was tight and slanted, filled with coded phrases—fragments that could have been case notes or confessions. One passage caught James's eye: *Every town hides its tithe. Pay the ones who keep the doors locked.*

A chill crept up his spine. "That sounds like blackmail."

Naomi nodded. "Or a payoff system. 'Tithe'—payments to ensure silence. The ledger may track them."

She flipped another page, revealing a list of initials paired with small amounts, none exceeding a few hundred dollars.

That night, Naomi returned to the café with her laptop. They sat again in his apartment, the soft glow of the screen lighting their faces as she scrolled through files recovered from Elena's flash drive. Most were encrypted, but a few text documents opened—fragments of messages, incomplete memos, scattered references to "Phase Two."

Naomi tapped one entry. "Look. She mentions transfers to the Ashwood Relief Fund. Ever heard of it?"

James nodded slowly. "It's a charity the town set up after the flood six years ago. Reverend Samuel Blake runs it."

Naomi leaned back. "Then we have our first connection between Elena's operation and the town's leadership."

"Reverend Blake," James said, the name turning sour in his mouth. "Everyone trusts him."

"That's what could make him powerful," Naomi replied. "If this ledger ties to that fund, we'll need to tread carefully."

She opened another file. Lines of numbers scrolled across the screen, each ending with a symbol from the ledger. "Whoever managed these accounts had a background in finance. Not Elena."

"The accomplice," James said.

Naomi looked up. "We'll find them. Together."

He met her gaze. "You really believe that?"

"I wouldn't be here otherwise."

A gust of wind rattled the windowpane. For a moment, they sat in silence, listening—the faint rumble of a distant truck, the creak of a shutter, the wind threading through the square.

Naomi reached for the ledger again and flipped to the final page. Her eyes narrowed. "Wait," she said. "This isn't random. Look. These letters at the bottom. Not currency. Not code."

James leaned over her shoulder. "Then what?"

"Initials," she said quietly. "People."

The final line read: 'Authorization complete – E.M. / S.B.'

Naomi's breath caught. "S.B.," she whispered.

James felt the blood drain from his face. "Elena wasn't the end of it."

Naomi closed the ledger and met his eyes. "No," she said. "It's the beginning of something much bigger than we understand."

Chapter 14 – A Town in Shadows

The fog rolled in before dawn, drifting off the Ashwood River and curling through the streets like something alive. By morning, the entire town was wrapped in it. Shops, lampposts, even the church spire disappeared into a soft gray nothing. It gave the illusion of quiet, but James knew better. Silence in Ashwood never meant peace. It meant preparation.

He stood by the café window, coffee cooling in his hand, watching blurred shapes pass on the street. Naomi sat at a small table, the ledger open before her, its coded pages spread across a map of Ashwood that she'd taped together from old town surveys.

"Whoever designed this cipher knew what they were doing," she said. "It's not random substitution. It's layered. Dates, letters, and symbols that shift depending on location."

James nodded slowly. "Elena liked puzzles. But this isn't her handwriting in the margins." He traced a finger along the notations written in a tighter, slanted script. "This is someone else's."

Naomi adjusted her glasses and leaned closer. "These entries, here and here, refer to transfers labeled A.R.F. I think that stands for the Ashwood Relief Fund. I checked the town's records last night. The fund's accounts show monthly withdrawals marked as 'maintenance reimbursements.'"

"Which is a polite way of saying someone's been siphoning money," James said.

Naomi's mouth tightened. "Exactly. The amounts aren't large enough to trigger state audits, but they add up over time. Hundreds of small transfers over six years."

He stared at the symbols again. "Elena didn't have access to those records. She wasn't an accountant. So how did she get these details?"

Naomi tapped the pen against her notebook. "Either someone inside the Relief Fund gave them to her, or she was working with someone who did."

"Someone like Reverend Blake," James said, the words heavier than he expected.

Naomi looked up. "You know him?"

"Everyone does. He's been here longer than anyone else on the council. He's respected and trusted." James hesitated.

He's worth a visit," Naomi said.

The fog thickened as they reached the church. Its white steeple rose faintly above the mist, a pale finger pointing heavenward. Inside, candles flickered near the altar, and the scent of old wood and wax hung in the air.

Reverend Samuel Blake was arranging hymnals when they entered. He turned with a smile that was warm, practiced, and perfectly measured.

"Detective Pierce," he said, extending a hand. "And Mr. Whitaker. I wondered when I'd see you again."

"Reverend," Naomi said politely. "Thank you for meeting us."

"Of course." He gestured for them to sit in the first pew. "I imagine this is about the Relief Fund. The council has already been in touch."

Naomi nodded. "Yes. I'm reviewing all accounts connected to Charles Redmond and any public foundations under his management."

Blake folded his hands. "A necessary precaution, I'm sure. It's been difficult, learning that one of our own officers betrayed the town's trust."

"Understandably," Naomi said. "You worked closely with Elena, didn't you?"

His smile faltered just slightly. "Insofar as any of us did. She consulted occasionally on matters of security, including grant distributions and verification procedures. She was efficient. Distant, but efficient."

James observed him carefully. "Did she ever mention the Relief Fund specifically? Or show interest in its finances?"

Blake's eyes flickered toward him. "Not to me. However, it wouldn't surprise me if she accessed those records. Officers often overstep boundaries in the name of justice."

Naomi said nothing for a moment, then closed her notebook. "Thank you, Reverend. I may have additional questions later."

He inclined his head graciously. "I'm always here to help."

They left the church, their footsteps muffled by the damp pavement. James exhaled once they were outside. "He's hiding something."

Naomi nodded. "Agreed. That momentary shift when you mentioned the Relief Fund. That wasn't surprise. That was calculation."

"He knows exactly what Elena was doing," James said.

"Which means," Naomi replied, "we have to find what she left behind before he, or whoever's working with him, destroys it."

Back at the café, Mae was wiping down tables when they returned. "You look like you've seen a ghost," she said.

Naomi accepted a cup of coffee and glanced toward the window. The fog had started to lift, revealing the pale outlines of parked cars. "Reverend Blake's composure worries me," she said quietly. "Men who are truly innocent don't rehearse their reactions that well."

Mae paused mid-wipe. "You think he's involved in all that mess Elena started?"

Naomi didn't answer directly. "I think Elena's ledger wasn't meant to expose her crimes. It was meant to document someone else's."

Mae crossed her arms. "Then maybe it's time this town stopped worshiping its false idols."

James looked at her sharply. "You've never liked Blake."

"I like what he pretends to be," Mae said. "But I've seen too many good people lose their homes while he collects donations to 'pray' for them. There's something hollow behind that smile."

Naomi nodded thoughtfully. "Then maybe you're the first person who actually sees him clearly."

Mae's eyes softened. "Just be careful, both of you. Elena fooled us all once. Whoever's left won't make the same mistake."

That evening, Naomi spread the ledger and notes across the café's back table. The overhead light hummed softly as she worked through patterns. James leaned beside her, tracing the connections between coded entries and bank withdrawal dates.

"I think these triangles," Naomi said, "represent recurring monthly payments. The circles might mean cash exchanges."

James studied one column. "And these initials beside the entries—M.L., C.R., and then S.B. They line up with known community figures."

Naomi frowned. "C.R.—Charles Redmond. M.L.—Maggie Lake, his accountant. That fits. But S.B. Are we back to Blake again?" She leaned back in her chair. "Every path loops back to him."

"And yet," James said quietly, "the deeper we look, the less evidence we can touch. It's all notes, codes, and signatures. Nothing solid."

"That's how professionals hide their crimes," Naomi said. "In plain sight, disguised as community service."

James rubbed his temples. "If Blake really was Elena's partner, he's clever enough to play both sides. He probably used her ambition, then planned to cut her loose when she became a liability."

Naomi closed the ledger. "If that's true, then we're dealing with someone who's always three steps ahead."

James glanced at the clock—it was almost midnight. "Maybe we should call it a night."

Naomi nodded reluctantly. "Get some rest. Tomorrow, I'll pull Blake's financials from the Relief Fund archives. If there's a paper trail, we'll find it."

Mae had gone home and left the cafe closing to James. When Naomi left, he locked the door and turned off the light, the café's neon sign buzzing faintly through the fog.

He didn't know it yet, but someone was watching from across the street.

James stood alone behind the counter with the lights dimmed, the ledger and Naomi's notes stacked neatly beneath the register. He turned the deadbolt, rattled it once, and peered through the pane in the door to make sure Main Street was empty.

Upstairs, his room waited with the stubborn familiarity of a place you never planned to live in for long. He flicked off the last light and climbed the back stairs. Halfway up, he stopped. A faint crunch sounded under his shoe. He lifted his foot and squinted. On the painted step was a crescent of silt, river grit that didn't belong there, pressed into a heel print that wasn't his. It pointed up toward his door.

He crouched, fingertips hovering over the print. The edges were soft, already blurring in the damp. The person who made it had come through recently, but not within the last few minutes. On the landing, he found a second mark just outside his door. He reached for the key, then paused and pressed his ear to the wood. Nothing. No whisper of steps, no rustle. He unlocked the door in one smooth motion, swung it inward, and stayed in the frame, letting his eyes sweep the room the way Elena had taught him, left to right, low to high, familiar to strange.

The familiar was all there. The desk with its careful stacks, the mug he had left near the lamp, and the coat draped over the chair were all as he had left them. The strange was small but stubborn. A pencil he kept parallel to the notebook lay at a diagonal. A book on the dresser, The Shipping News, sat a finger's width forward from its neighbors. The window latch, which he had checked twice earlier, stood at an angle that said someone had tested it and found it stuck. Whoever had come hadn't stayed long.

He left the door open and crossed to the desk. The drawer was unchanged. The folder weight felt the same. The ledger was downstairs, safe.

His phone buzzed. Naomi: *Home. Lab confirms ledger ink is from two hands: Elena and an unknown person. Also, ARF audit request filed. Sleep if you can.* He texted back: *Footprints on back stairs. Someone was in my room. Nothing missing.* Naomi replied. *Do not engage alone.* He typed, *Copy,* and put the phone face down so he wouldn't be tempted to say anything braver than he felt. He rechecked the landing, then closed and locked the door. For long minutes he stood without moving. He made tea he didn't want and carried it to the window. Condensation filmed the glass. He drew a small circle with his thumb and looked down. For a moment, he saw his own reflection, a man in a gray sweater holding a cup with both hands like a supplicant. He set the cup down harder than he meant to.

He should have slept. Instead he pulled out his legal pad and began writing the day's events. He listed the patterns Naomi had teased from the ledger: triangles for monthly payments, circles for cash, squares for transfers that corresponded to the Relief Fund ledger. He wrote S.B. in the margin.

A slight sound down the stairs lifted the hair along his arms. Not the clank of the café's pipes. Not Mae's purposeful step. A lighter rhythm, tap, pause, tap, like weight testing wood. He crossed the room and clicked off the lamp. The sound again: not quite a footfall, not quite a knock. He slid the chain free and eased the door open a hand's width. He waited, letting his eyes drink the gray until shadow deepened into shape. Nothing moved. The stairwell smelled like damp wood and metal. Somewhere, far off, a train stitched the dark with a line of sound.

He stepped out and let the door close gently behind him. "Hello?" Quiet, almost conversational. No answer. "If this is a joke, it isn't funny." He descended one step, then another. On the second-to-last tread, he saw it. There was a thin line directly in front of the doorframe at eye level. He frowned and reached out. Something hung there, suspended by a nearly invisible length of fishing line that quivered when the stair vibrated under his weight. He followed it with his eyes to the door's center.

He saw the black first, then the shape. A crow. The head lolled at an unnatural angle, beak parted as if mid-cry. A scrap of paper was tacked to the door. For a beat, he didn't move. His stomach lifted and settled. He took the last step slowly, giving himself time to turn revulsion into observation. The bird was fresh. There was no smell yet, and the feathers were unruffled. He reached for the paper and paused. Gloves. He went back up two steps, fished the thin latex pair from the hall kit he kept out of habit, tugged them on, and returned. The paper tore free. Three words in block letters stared up at him.

You should have stopped with Elena.

He read it twice, then once more, because repetition made reality set in. The words carried no flourish and no signature. The block letters were neat without fussy alignment, the kind you learn when you're taught to print in school.

"Message received," he said to the fog, quietly angry. He photographed the scene from three angles, then two close-ups of the tack and the note's message. He texted Naomi one photograph and nothing else, knowing she would call him.

The phone vibrated immediately. "Tell me you're not standing there alone," Naomi said, voice flattened by distance but sharp with urgency.

"I am. But only for a minute." He let the facts come out plain. "Dead Crow hanging from fishing line. Note nailed to door.

"Do not touch anything else," she said. "I'm on my way. Ten minutes." A breath, then softer, "James. Keep the door in sight and keep your back to a wall."

He smiled despite himself. "Copy, Detective."

He didn't like leaving the crow there, but preserving the scene mattered. He stepped back, putting the corner of the landing against his shoulder, and let the darkness be his cover. He listened, not for footsteps now, but for the absence of them

Someone must have been hiding in the cafe as he was locking up.

Headlights softened the fog at the mouth of the lane and then sharpened as a sedan eased in without drama. Naomi stepped out wearing a dark field jacket, with her hair braided tightly and a small kit in her hand. She didn't waste words. A nod for him, then she moved to the door and crouched, reading the scene at a pace that matched his own.

"They centered the tack," she murmured. "Measured? Or just an eye for it."

"Not a kid," she agreed. "Not a drunk." She photographed the note, bagged it with tweezers, working quickly but not rushed. "We'll get DNA off the tack if we're lucky. Prints, maybe, if no gloves were worn. The line's mass-market. You can buy it at any hardware or bait shop." She rose and gave him the look she reserved for truths she knew he would hate.

Naomi tilted her head toward the stairs. They climbed to his room while she called the on-call tech. With a clipped voice, she gave the address, itemization, and chain-of-custody instructions. Inside, she took the seat by the window and set her kit on the desk. "We'll put a patrol at the front and one rolling the block," she said. "It won't catch a ghost, but it'll make the living hesitate."

He leaned against the dresser, arms folded to keep them from shaking. Now that she was here, the delayed tremor had permission to arrive. He lifted a shoulder. "They were inside earlier. Small signs. A pencil moved, a book pulled. I think they were looking for the ledger.

"They'll assume it's with you sometimes," she said. "And that you get tired and sloppy. It's what I would assume, if I were them." She angled toward him. "Listen to me. Whoever did that downstairs is escalating. They will try to make you afraid enough to stop or angry enough to make mistakes. You will do neither."

A quiet settled between them, not comfortable, not hostile, something like a pact. Naomi stood. " I want you to sleep with the chain on. In the morning, we'll follow the keys, pull the Relief Fund subledgers, and speak with two people: Mae and Reverend Blake. No widening the circle. No broadcast."

She slung the kit over her shoulder. At the door, she paused, hand on the frame, and looked back. "They chose a crow," she said. "A bird that recognizes faces. Remember that."

He listened to her steps fade down the stairs, to the low exchange with the arriving techs, to the careful words professionals use when they take ugliness into custody. He turned off the lamp, went to the window and thought of the message on the note. *You should have stopped with Elena.* The note was gone to evidence, but its sentence remained inside him, neat and implacable as block print.

"Not a chance."

Chapter 15 – Whispers and Warnings

The next morning, the fog returned to Ashwood like a bad habit that refused to break. James Whitaker walked beside Detective Naomi Pierce through the damp air to the town office, their steps echoing on the slick pavement.

Naomi's tone was low but deliberate. "We discovered Victor Lane handled nearly every account Redmond touched—the Relief Fund, the estate holdings, and even the church renovations."

James nodded, tightening his coat. "Then he's the link. The only one with access to both sides of the ledger."

They turned onto an older street lined with dark storefronts and lamplight pooling on the wet cobblestones. "He left town right after Elena's arrest," Naomi continued. "No trace, no forwarding address. But his name keeps appearing in Redmond's financial records."

James glanced toward her. "You think he helped her?"

"I think he was the one who made it possible," she said. "She knew how to manipulate people. He knew how to hide the proof."

He almost smiled. "Two halves of the same con."

When they entered the office, the archives smelled of paste and paper dust—the scent of old secrets kept too long. Henry Doyle, the town clerk, looked up from a leaning tower of ledgers when they entered.

"Detective Pierce," he said, adjusting his glasses. "You wanted access to the Relief Fund accounts?"

Naomi smiled politely. "And anything connected to Victor Lane."

The man shuffled through folders until he found a thin bundle. "Lane was tidy. Every number is as neat as handwriting in a prayer book. People trusted him because he looked like someone who should be trusted."

James leaned closer. "When did he leave Ashwood?"

"After Elena Marquez was arrested," Doyle said. "Said he had family up north. Never sold his house, though. Taxes are still paid—cashier's checks, from different banks each quarter."

Naomi's pen paused. "Who oversaw the Relief Fund during that time?"

"Reverend Blake," Doyle said. "Lane handled the bookkeeping, and the Reverend made the announcements. Between them, the town thought their money was saving souls."

James frowned. "And was it?"

Doyle sighed. "Depends on whose soul you mean."

Naomi thanked him and stepped outside, her expression unreadable. The drizzle had thickened, clinging to their coats.

"Blake's name keeps surfacing," James said quietly.

"Then we'll find out why," Naomi replied.

Mulberry Street glistened under the rain, each puddle reflecting blurred lamplight. Midway down the lane stood a narrow house with drawn curtains and a faded for-sale sign.

Naomi studied it. "Mailbox is clean. Someone empties it."

James leaned closer to the window. The faint silhouette of furniture sat untouched inside. "If Lane's gone, he left his life behind."

Naomi's phone buzzed. She turned away to answer. "Pierce." She listened, then frowned. "Send it to me."

When she hung up, her tone had changed. "The bank flagged a dormant Relief Fund account. Someone withdrew five thousand dollars yesterday using Lane's credentials."

James raised an eyebrow. "After all this time?"

"Either he's back," she said, "or someone's using his name as cover."

Naomi's gaze lingered on the dark house. "Either way, he's close. I think it's time to have that discussion with Mae and Blake."

By late afternoon, the café's golden windows felt like a sanctuary. Mae looked up from behind the counter, flour streaking her apron. "You two look like you've been walking through dense fog."

"Right," James said, shaking the damp from his coat.

Naomi showed her a photo of Victor Lane. "Have you seen this man around lately?"

Mae studied the image. "Victor? Used to sit in that booth every Thursday, right where you're standing. Always ordered oatmeal and coffee, always paid in cash."

James blinked. "So he left quietly after Elena's arrest?"

Mae gave a slow nod. "People like him just fade until you stop looking."

Naomi smiled faintly. "If he turns up again, please call me."

Mae set the photo down. "If I do, I'll pour him coffee but not conversation."

As James reached for his cup, Mae's tone softened. "You two are chasing that Relief Fund now, aren't you?"

Naomi met her eyes. "You know about it?"

Mae snorted. "Who doesn't? Everyone in Ashwood donated when it started. We thought we were helping factory families after it closed down. Reverend Blake preached about compassion every Sunday."

James leaned forward. "Did the money ever reach those families?"

"Some," Mae said. "Enough to look legitimate. After the first year, though, no one mentioned it anymore. You know how this town works—truth only lasts until it makes someone uncomfortable."

Naomi wrote something down. "Did you ever see Lane or Blake meeting?"

Mae nodded. "Plenty. Right there in that corner booth. Looked more like confession than accounting."

James and Naomi exchanged a look.

When Mae brought their coffee to the table, her eyes lingered on Naomi a moment longer than usual. "You ever find answers that just make more questions?" she asked quietly.

Naomi smiled faintly. "That's most of my career."

Mae nodded, wiping her hands on her apron. "You and Reverend Blake stopped in here not long ago. Separate visits, same week. The funny thing was, neither of you seemed to want the other to know."

Naomi looked up. "Reverend Blake came by?"

"Twice," Mae said. "Once to ask if you'd said anything about him, and once to tell me how grateful the church was for my donations." Her tone carried a hint of skepticism. "Strange how those two things fit in the same breath."

James set his cup down. "What did you tell him?"

"The truth," Mae said. "That I don't keep secrets for anyone but my customers' recipes." She hesitated, then added, "But he made a statement that stuck with me. He said sometimes sin doesn't look like greed or anger. It looks like persistence. I'm not sure what he meant, but it didn't sound like a sermon."

Naomi's pen had appeared almost unconsciously, scratching a quick note. "He's watching how far we're willing to push."

Mae gave a dry laugh. "Maybe he's afraid you'll push him over."

As they rose to leave, Mae touched James's sleeve. "That night you came to ask about Elena," she said softly, "you told me truth leaves marks, even when people try to hide it. You were right. But so does fear. Watch yourself, James."

He managed a small smile. "That's becoming a theme around here."

Mae's gaze flicked briefly toward the church steeple visible through the window. "Then maybe it's time you started listening to your own advice."

"Thank you, Mae," Naomi said gently. "You've helped more than you know."

"Just don't bring trouble back to my door," Mae said, forcing a small smile. "Ashwood's had enough ghosts lately."

The church stood at the far end of the square, its windows glowing faintly through the fog. When they entered, candlelight shimmered against polished brass, and the air smelled faintly of rain-soaked hymnals.

Reverend Blake appeared from a side hallway, his steps measured, his presence calm. "Detective Pierce. Mr. Whitaker. Always a pleasure, though I sense this isn't a social visit."

Naomi returned the faint smile. "We're reviewing the Relief Fund records. Thought we'd hear about it from the man who announced it."

Blake's expression didn't change. "Ah, a noble cause. Those funds kept more than a few families from ruin."

James stepped forward. "According to the records, transfers were made from accounts managed by Victor Lane. You worked closely?"

"Mr. Lane is an honest man," Blake said smoothly. "Thorough. I trusted him with the details."

Naomi's tone remained polite but cool. "Did you ever review the accounts yourself?"

He chuckled softly. "Detective, if faith can't extend to finances, what hope is there for the soul?"

James studied him. "Elena trusted you, too. She mentioned your counsel more than once."

Blake's eyes flickered. "Elena was troubled. But redemption often walks hand in hand with guilt. You of all people should know that, Mr. Whitaker."

The words landed with quiet precision, like a sermon wrapped in warning.

Naomi closed her notebook. "If you think of anything that might help us locate Victor Lane, please contact me."

Blake inclined his head, the gesture slow and deliberate. "Of course. And if you find yourselves seeking solace instead of suspects, you'll always be welcome here."

Outside, the church bell tolled six times. Through the glass, James saw Blake still standing in the doorway, watching them go, and he wasn't smiling anymore.

That night, James worked at his desk, pages of notes spread in careful rows. Each name—Redmond, Margaret, Elena, Blake, and Lane—seemed to twist back on itself.

He leaned back, rubbing his temples. Below, the faint clink of dishes told him Mae was closing up.

He turned to gather his papers and froze. The desk drawer was open a fraction of an inch.

He hadn't left it that way.

He pulled it open. The folders were neatly stacked, but his voice recorder was gone. In its place lay something metallic, gleaming softly.

Elena Marquez's badge.

The sight hit him like a punch. Her nameplate glinted under the light, scratched but unmistakable.

He grabbed his phone, heart pounding. "Naomi," he said when she answered. "Someone's been here. They took my recorder and left something behind."

"What?"

"Elena's badge."

There was silence, then her voice sharpened. "Don't touch it. I'm on my way."

Fifteen minutes later, Naomi stepped inside, rain darkening her hair. She crouched beside the desk, examining the badge with gloved hands. "Clean," she said quietly. "No prints. They knew exactly what message they were sending."

"Which is?" James asked.

"That Elena's ghost still has reach."

He gave a low laugh. "Or that someone wants me to think so."

Naomi stood, her gaze steady. "Either way, they're watching us. So let them. I'd rather see their eyes than their shadow."

James's unease lingered..

Somewhere outside, the foghorn moaned over the river, long and low.

Ashwood wasn't sleeping.

Chapter 16 – A Dangerous Game

The next morning, a thick veil of fog still hung over the town, softening the edges of every building and turning streetlights into pale, trembling orbs. James leaned against the passenger door of Naomi Pierce's sedan. He hadn't slept much. Every sound of tires on wet pavement felt like it might belong to someone watching them.

Naomi sat in the driver's seat, her expression composed and focused. They were observing Victor Lane's house. "He's on schedule," she murmured, adjusting the binoculars. "That makes three mornings in a row."

James took a sip from his cooling coffee. "People who disappear like to believe they're still predictable. Routine makes them feel invisible."

Naomi smirked faintly. "You sound like a cop."

He shook his head. "Just a man who's been invisible before."

Through the fog, they saw the narrow door of the Mulberry Street house open. A man stepped out, shoulders hunched, a briefcase clutched close to his chest. Victor Lane—known now to his neighbors as Daniel Voss—walked with the cautious precision of a man expecting to be followed.

"There he is," Naomi whispered.

James jotted the time in his notebook. "Same coat, same path."

Naomi started the car. "Let's see if he leads us somewhere new."

The drive was slow and deliberate. The mist swallowed the road as if they were moving through a dream. Houses slipped past, silent witnesses behind curtained windows.

"He's not heading to the bank," Naomi said. "Too far east."

James squinted through the fog. "Industrial district."

The one with the old hardware store?"

"If you wanted to meet someone in private, that's the spot. Half the block's condemned."

Naomi's fingers drummed once on the steering wheel. "Then that's where we'll find him."

She parked two streets away. The quiet was so complete it pressed on their eardrums. James caught the faint scent of oil and rain-damp rust. Somewhere, a lone crow cawed and fell silent.

Naomi reached for her shoulder holster, checking the magazine. "If this goes wrong, you fall back. Clear?"

"I've seen worse," he said.

"Not in Ashwood, you haven't."

He smiled faintly but didn't argue.

The old hardware store stood dilapidated at the edge of the street, its windows opaque with grime. A sign, half-detached above the door, read "Hollister & Sons Hardware," the letters half-hidden beneath the dirt.

Naomi gestured for silence. They slipped down the side alley, boots quiet on the slick concrete. Through a cracked pane of glass, they saw him. Victor Lane bent over a worktable beneath a single hanging bulb, its light swinging slightly as if disturbed by his shaking hands.

Naomi whispered, "He's packing documents."

James leaned closer. "Or destroying them."

"Let's make sure he doesn't."

She eased the side door open. It groaned softly, but Lane was too absorbed in his work to hear. They stepped inside, moving between old shelving units draped in cobwebs.

The smell hit first—mold, dust, and something chemical, sharp in the throat.

Naomi spoke evenly. "Victor Lane."

He froze. The pen fell from his fingers and rolled across the floor. Slowly, he turned. His face was hollow, unshaven, his eyes bloodshot.

"I'm not armed," he said hoarsely.

"Then we're already getting along," Naomi said. "Why are you here?"

He looked from her to James and back again, his chest rising fast. "You wouldn't believe me."

"Try us," James said quietly.

Lane's voice cracked. "I didn't start this. I thought I was helping."

Naomi stepped closer. "Helping who?"

"Reverend Blake," he whispered. "The Relief Fund. He said it was to rebuild Ashwood, to heal what Redmond's greed had broken. Then the money started going to shell accounts—large amounts, untraceable. I questioned it once. He told me faith required obedience."

"Did Elena obey too?" Naomi asked.

Lane's shoulders sagged. "She believed him. He convinced her she was cleansing sin, not creating it. When Redmond found out, she thought killing him was divine justice."

James's stomach turned. "And you? What was your role in God's bookkeeping?"

Lane gave a bitter laugh. "I balanced the ledgers. I made the lies neat enough to look true."

Naomi's gaze hardened. "Then you can help us unmake them. Where's the evidence?"

He gestured toward the metal boxes on the table–eight of them. "In those. I was going to burn the contents tonight."

"Not anymore. They look locked. How were you going to open them?"

"I have duplicate keys. Elena had another set".

Inside the boxes lay thick ledgers, sealed envelopes, and a stack of blank passports. James opened one and saw the crisp watermark—perfect forgeries.

"Forged identities," he said. "For who?"

Lane hesitated. "For all of us. In case the storm came. Blake said righteousness had a price, and sometimes you had to buy your way out of it."

Naomi flipped open the first ledger. Coded entries filled each page with numbers, dates, and initials. She pointed to one. "S.B."

"Samuel Blake," Lane whispered. "He built the network. Redmond's empire was just the foundation. Elena enforced it. I made it invisible."

"Why come back?" James asked. "Why risk being found?"

Lane swallowed hard. "Because guilt doesn't let you sleep. And because I knew Blake wouldn't stop until every loose thread was cut."

Naomi lowered the ledger. "Including you."

He nodded miserably.

A sound interrupted them—a faint metallic clink from the back of the store.

Naomi froze. "What was that?"

Lane's eyes widened. "He found me."

"Who?"

Before anyone could answer, the rear corridor erupted in flame.

The explosion wasn't massive, but it was close enough to force them into motion. Shelves toppled. The light bulb burst overhead. The ledgers, envelopes and passports flew everywhere. Naomi shoved Lane toward the door, shouting, "Go!"

Heat rolled across the room in waves. James grabbed what ledgers he could salvage, coughing as smoke filled his lungs. The air stung with the burning smell of varnish and rust.

"Move!" Naomi called. "Follow my voice!"

They stumbled through the haze. The wooden planks beneath their feet creaked and snapped. Lane tripped once; James pulled him up, eyes watering from the smoke. At last they burst through the side door into the alley, gulping cold air. Behind them, flames crawled up the building's walls, feeding greedily on dry wood.

Lane leaned against the brick, gasping. "Everything's gone," he croaked. "You don't know what you've taken."

Naomi held the saved ledgers against her chest. "I think we have an idea."

He shook his head violently. "No. You don't. Those books name people who'd bury this whole town to stay hidden. You can't fight them."

"We already are," James said.

Lane's mouth opened as if to argue, then snapped shut as a bullet struck the wall inches from his head.

"Down!" Naomi barked, pulling both men low.

Another shot cracked through the fog, ricocheting off a metal bin.

Naomi drew her gun. "Sniper—rooftop!"

James could hear his pulse louder than the gunfire. "You see him?"

She fired twice into the haze. No return shot. Just silence and the roar of the burning building.

"He's repositioning," she said. "We move!" They bolted down the alley, orange light chasing them. Smoke bled into fog until the world became one shifting blur. When they reached the corner, Naomi shoved Lane into the shelter of a doorway.

"Talk!" she demanded. "Who's helping Blake?"

Lane's lips trembled. "You wouldn't believe me."

"Try anyway."

He inhaled sharply, ready to speak—then jerked as his body convulsed.

The crack of the rifle echoed half a second later.

"Lane!" James caught him as he fell. Blood bloomed across his chest, hot and slick.

Naomi ducked beside them, eyes scanning the rooftops. "East building! Third-floor window!"

She fired back twice, but the shooter was gone. The only movement came from the flickering flames.

James pressed his hand against the wound, but the light was already leaving Lane's eyes. "Stay with me," he whispered.

Lane's lips moved. "It's bigger than Blake." Then his body went still.

Naomi checked for a pulse. Nothing.

She swore softly, then reached into his jacket, pulling out a folded note sealed with wax. "He was trying to give us something."

James looked up, the fire roaring higher behind them. "And now he's proof that we're next."

By the time the fire trucks arrived, half the block was glowing orange through the fog. The air hissed with steam as water hit the walls, turning to mist before it could reach the wood. Naomi and James stood at the police line, both coated in soot, watching the flames devour the last of the evidence.

James's voice was low. "We had him. He wanted to talk."

"He did talk," Naomi said. "Just not enough."

He turned toward her, frustration tightening his voice. "He mentioned others—a council, the bank. What if this thing runs through the whole town?"

Naomi's expression didn't change. "Then we cut deeper."

They watched as a charred piece of timber collapsed, sending up a burst of sparks. The smell of wet ash settled heavily in the fog. For a long moment, neither spoke.

Then James noticed it. A shadow moved beyond the barrier tape, too steady to be a bystander. Tall, broad-shouldered, walking calmly through the mist. "Naomi," he said quietly. "By the lamppost."

She followed his gaze just as the figure turned its head slightly. Even through the haze, the posture and calm gait were unmistakable.

"Blake," she whispered.

"He wanted us to see him."

"He's cleaning house," Naomi said grimly. "And he's not done."

James watched until the Reverend's figure dissolved into the fog. "You realize what this means."

"That he's losing control?"

"No," James said softly. "That he thinks he hasn't."

A gust of wind swept down the street, bending the smoke into ghostly shapes. The fire hissed one last time as the final wall caved in, sparks spiraling skyward. Somewhere far off, the church bell began to toll—slow and deliberate—echoing through the mist.

Neither of them moved until the sound faded. Then they returned to the car.

Chapter 17 – Friends or Foes

In town, people walked more softly, as if the sound itself might shatter something fragile. Blinds were half-drawn along Main, faces a blur behind glass, mouths moving in small, urgent shapes. By noon, Victor Lane had died three different ways, according to rumor.

James Whitaker and Detective Naomi Pierce crossed the square without speaking.

They're talking," James said at last.

"They always do," Naomi answered, eyes never leaving the courthouse door. "What's the theme this time?"

"That you're cursed," he said.

Naomi stopped. Gray light turned her irises into slate. "When I worked arson in Dover," she said calmly, "a suspect killed himself the night before trial. The papers called me the Black Widow. 'Justice dies where she walks.' People like curses. Curses are tidy." I don't have time to worry about what people say about me. I prefer to gather facts."

"Then let's collect some," James said, falling in beside her.

Inside Mae's cafe, the bell over the door gave a thin, apologetic chime. The morning crowd had thinned to a murmur. Only two farmers hunched over eggs, a pair of teachers whispering at the window, and a newspaper left folded on a corner table were all that remained.

Mae stood behind the counter, drying a clean glass. She took one look at them and set the towel aside. "Coffee first," she said. "Talking after."

"Both sound good," James said.

She poured, slid the mugs across, then lowered her voice. "Blake came in early. Sat there an hour with his hands folded. Didn't order. Told me he was praying for Ashwood's soul."

James angled his head toward the window. "You think he knows we're closing in?"

"I think he's already decided what to do about it," Mae said. "Men like that don't wait for the Lord's will. They write it."

"If he comes back, call me. Not after. During."

Later, across town in her temporary office, Naomi had turned paper into landscape. Ledgers, maps, photographs, and transcripts lay in ordered stacks. The corkboard on the wall bristled with red string like a stitched wound. Charles Redmond. Elena Marquez. Victor Lane. Reverend Samuel Blake. Beneath them, a column of council photos of Holloway, Cobb, Reed, and two others.

James stood at the window while Naomi decoded another line of the ledger.

"You ever get the feeling this town is alive?" he asked. "Like it knows when you're trying to expose it."

"It's been alive a long time," she said, pen scratching. "Sick, too. We're just naming the infection."

"Blake's everywhere," he said. "Church, charities, council. He's the bloodstream."

"Then we go for the heart," Naomi said simply. "The council. They signed the authorizations Lane laundered."

He turned from the window. "Do you trust any of them?"

"No," she said. "Silence is guilt until proven otherwise."

He half-smiled. "That's a prosecutor's line." "It's a survivor's," she said.

He watched her a beat longer, then asked, "What happens to you when this is over?"

She blinked once, as if surprised he'd aimed the question at her. "They transfer me somewhere that needs a mess cleaned."

"That's logistics," he said. "I meant you."

She capped her pen and leaned back. "You want history, Whitaker? All right." She pointed at the board without looking. "When I was nineteen, my mother's brother died in custody. The department called it a fall. The bruises on his ribs weren't from falling. No one investigated. No one apologized. I started at the academy the following year and learned how to read a room where the truth wasn't welcome. Later, in another precinct, evidence disappeared for a councilman's son. I filed an internal report. They called me disloyal."

James said nothing for a moment. "So you learned not to trust uniforms."

"I learned not to trust power," she said. "Uniforms just hide it better."

He leaned against the sill. "My turn."

Her eyebrows rose. "I didn't ask."

"You were about to," he said, and the smallest piece of color returned to her face.

"My parents ran a hardware store two blocks from Hollister & Sons," he said. "Before the mill died, the whole town smelled like sawdust. After, it smelled like loss. We survived on fix-it parts and credit. Folks used to come in to buy a nail and leave with a confession. I got good at listening. I thought that meant journalism.

I went to D.C., then abroad to wars, earthquakes, and elections. People lied to themselves in bigger fonts." He rubbed at a nick on the window frame. "An editor told me readers wanted hope more than truth. I told him they'd settle for honesty. He told me to write a lifestyle column. I quit instead."

Naomi's tone softened around the edges. "And came back to Ashwood because?"

"My cousin's engagement," he said. "And because leaving doesn't erase the shape of a place in you. Then Redmond died, and I didn't recognize my hometown anymore."   I keep writing because I need the world to make sense. You keep working because you refuse to let it not."

"Don't analyze me," she said, but without bite.

"Occupational hazard."

"Mine is staying alive," she said. "Which is why you're going to hear me when I say this next part. "You're useful," Naomi said. "People talk to you because you belong here and somehow yet don't. If Blake can't scare you, he'll smear you. A discredited reporter is as good as a dead one to men like him."

James breathed out through his nose. "You're telling me to be careful."

"I'm telling you to let me be the one they shoot at first," she said, perfectly even. "I know how to wear armor. You know how to write. We each do our part."

He studied her. "When this is done, I'm going to pretend I didn't hear the part where you volunteer to get shot at."

"Pretend all you want," she said. "You heard me."

He smiled, then let it fade. "So. Council?"

"I called an emergency session for tonight," Naomi said, uncapping the pen again. "Holloway agreed. They'll expect an update on the fire. We'll give them math."

"And if Blake is there?"

"Then he hears the bell tolling for him from my mouth," she said.

The afternoon fled by. James went back to his room to shower the smoke out of his hair. He went to get his recorder from the desk, then remembered it was gone, stolen and replaced with a badge like a ghost. He picked up a pen instead.

Downstairs, Mae boxed tomorrow's croissants and hummed to the radio. When James came down for a refill, she folded his hand around the mug like passing a charm against bad luck.

Later that evening, Naomi and James went to the courthouse, climbed the stairs in silence, their footfalls swallowed by the damp. "You stay behind me," she said softly at the door. "You watch hands, not faces."

"You think one of them will try something in the room?" he asked.

"I think one of them already has a list," she said.

They entered to the sound of their own breath and the tick of an old wall clock. The chamber stretched long and pale beneath dull chandeliers. Five officials sat along the polished table. Mayor Addison Holloway occupied the center like a modest monarch. On his right, sat Councilwoman Harriet Cobb, with her pearls twisted tight between her fingers, and Gregory Reed, broad and ruddy, the kind of banker who believed God loved balanced budgets.On his left sat two others whose names (Stone, Teller) James could never quite remember.

Conversations fell silent. Every head turned toward Naomi.

"Detective Pierce," Holloway said with varnished calm. "We appreciate your alacrity. The town needs reassurance."

"Then I'll be brief," Naomi said. She set a folder on the table, not theatrical, just final. "What burned at the hardware store was evidence. The fire was not an accident. Victor Lane did not die by chance. And the money that moved through the Ashwood Relief Fund did not bless this town." She slid the ledgers across the wood. "It bought silence."

Reed laughed once, ugly and too loud. "This is an outrage."

James stepped forward just enough to be a presence. "Outrage is what the families of your charity were owed," he said.

"Mr. Whitaker," Holloway said with the patience of a man who collects paperweights, "you have no standing here."

"I have eyes," James said.

Cobb spoke, brittle. "Detective, these numbers must be a misunderstanding. Reverend Blake personally—"

"Approved the transfers," Naomi said. "Lane kept the codes and initials. Redmond bankrolled. Elena enforced. Blake sanctified. You signed."

Holloway's tone cooled. "Be careful, Detective. You are accusing elected officials based on ledgers recovered from a crime scene."

James watched hands, like she'd told him, not expressions. Reed's fingers trembled as they reached for his cup and took a sip. Sweat slicked the man's temple, though the room was cool.

"You all right, Councilman?" James asked, almost gently.

Reed's eyes cut to him, contempt flaring, and then his throat worked. He lurched to his feet, clawing at his collar. He grasped the table as he began to fall and a water glass slid. It hit the table, rolled, and shattered on the floor with a sound that seemed to split the room.

"EMS!" Someone shouted, voice strangled.

Naomi was already moving. She caught Reed before he hit the floor, turning him on his side. Foam pearled at the corners of his mouth; a bitter almond smell bit the air.

"Cyanide," James said, the word tasting like metal.

Naomi's gaze flicked to the pitcher. It was untouched, then to the cup, with a ring of residue where his lips had been. "Brought his own," she said.

Harriet Cobb made a slight animal sound and covered her mouth. Holloway staggered back, one hand to the table as if he needed the town's furniture to keep him upright.

"God help us," he whispered.

"God didn't put something in the drink," Naomi said, rising. Her voice reached the back corners of the room, quiet and absolute. "No one leaves."

The chamber clerk hesitated. When she repeated herself, he crossed the room and drove the bolt home with a sound that startled everyone.

James stood very still and let his reporter's brain process the sequences. There was Reed's personal cup, the glass shattering on the floor, cyanide and a dead body on the floor. He looked at Naomi and saw that the soft places they'd shown each other upstairs were gone. She was a stern, professional detective again.

"This is what happens," she said, each word deliberate, "when you play both sides of a lie. You think Blake is protecting you? He is erasing you. One by one."

Cobb began to weep openly, pearls clacking against the table as her hands shook.

"You had chances," Naomi said. "All of you. You chose quiet." She let the sentence hang. "Now the loud part begins. Naomi's gaze traveled the table, face by face, not lingering long enough to be read. "Elena Marquez did not do this alone," she said softly. "When she fell, someone kept it running. That someone is here."

"Bring me the list of everyone who entered this building in the last hour." She said to the clerk. The clerk ran.

James looked at the faces again. But hands still told more than mouths. Cobb was gripping her pearls until her knuckles blanched. Holloway's fingers were worrying the edge of a blotter. The other two councilmen had their palms pressed flat to the tabletop as if they could hold stillness down and make it behave.

Naomi lowered her voice so only the room could hear. "Friends or foes," she said. "We'll decide which before the night is over."

Chapter 18 – Behind Closed Doors

Naomi crouched beside the body once more, her movements deliberate, economical. She lifted the councilman's wrist, confirmed what she already knew, and then set his hand down with the respect you give to a man you don't forgive but won't desecrate. When she stood, the whole room rose a fraction with her.

"Detective—" Mayor Holloway began, but the word broke in the middle and fell.

"Sit," Naomi said. The single syllable pinned him to his chair.

The chamber door opened and the clerk slipped back into the room, breathless, clutching a narrow ledger. "Sign-in book, ma'am. For the last two hours." His eyes kept cutting toward Reed and then away again.

Naomi told the clerk to rebolt the door, then took the ledger and flipped through the pages. "Councilmembers Holloway, Cobb, Stone, Teller, Whitman, and Reed," she read quietly. "Two staffers. One custodian. No clergy. No guests." She closed the book. "No one enters or leaves until the medical examiner and the state investigators arrive."

No one moved.

The clock ticked once, then again, each second louder than the last.

Naomi didn't raise her voice. She didn't need to. "Phones on the table. Now."

There was a murmured rustle of protest, but the metallic scrape of the bolt and the knowledge of the body on the tile kept it low. One by one, they produced their devices. Naomi slid the phones to James. "Photograph the lock screens with time. Then airplane mode." Her tone left no space for discussion.

"Detective," Harriet Cobb whispered, voice raw, "I swear to you. If I signed anything, I believed it was proper. The Reverend said the Relief Fund was—"

"Righteous?" Naomi supplied.

Harriet's chin trembled.

"Necessary." Naomi's eyes softened a hair, then hardened. "The signature is the same whether you closed your eyes or not." She gestured toward the ruined glass. "Do you see what your necessary has purchased?"

Holloway's hands worried the edge of a blotter. "Reed was under strain," he said. "His health—"

"Poison doesn't care about headaches," Naomi said.

A collective flinch moved over their faces. The idea landed. This was not an accident, not a freak echo of Daniel's death, but a message carefully arranged for them.

James felt the room tilt around that realization. Fear has an odor and it rose off the table like steam. He scanned hands, as she'd taught him, who gripped, who hid, who picked at invisible threads. Cobb clenched her pearls so hard the string might snap. Stone pressed his palms flat as if he could keep the surface from rippling. Teller rubbed the web of skin between thumb and forefinger, a small self-punishment with rhythm.

Naomi moved to the water service. She didn't touch the pitcher. She studied the rim, the condensation and the clean ring where it had sat undisturbed. "Reed's cup was prepped before he arrived," she said. "We'll confirm with lab results, but I'm telling you now. This wasn't poured in the room."

"Then who—" Cobb began.

"The accomplice," Naomi said, almost gently. "The one Elena relied on when she couldn't be in two places at once.

A shiver passed through her audience. It was the first time she'd said the word accomplice as if it had a specific face.

Naomi pointed to the staffers seated along the side wall. "Names."

"Dwayne," said the clerk who'd run the ledger. He held his spine straight. "And Ned." He nodded at the custodian, a wiry man with a face carved by labor.

"How long were you in this room before the council arrived?" Naomi asked.

"Thirty minutes," Dwayne said. "Setting the folders, water, and agendas. Ned checked the lights and cleared a maintenance ticket on the east hinge."

"You see anyone near Reed's seat?"

Dwayne's eyes darted to the spot as if he could replay time with focus. "I set a pad there. The cup was already at his place.

Ned scrubbed a hand over his jaw. "I saw no one, Detective. Anyone could have slid in and out while I was in the closet working on the hinge."

"Be specific," Naomi said. "Anyone with keys?"

"Half the building," he said. "The council, the clerk's desk, and Reverend Blake sometimes. He runs evening vigils here."

Blake had keys to the house where the town pretended to be at its best.

Movement at the window caught James's eye. Behind the haze, he counted silhouettes gathering on the steps. There were bowed heads, hands knitted, and bodies swaying in a gentle tide of shared purpose. A sign lifted, then dipped. He couldn't read it through the blur, and maybe that was merciful.

He found Naomi's gaze; she found his. The Reverend was building a prayer to catch the news cameras. A town on its knees while the council chamber locked itself from truth.

From the corridor, a firm knock. James opened the door and Sergeant Les, a veteran's steadiness in his shoulders, entered. "ME's here," he said. "Your call on moving the body."

"Photograph, then bag," Naomi said, already moving. "Keep his cup separate from everything else. Gloves on anyone who breathes near it. And Les, pull security cam footage from the east and south halls for the last hour."

Les nodded. "Already got IT (Information Technology) on it."

"Good. And," She pitched her voice lower. "Watch the Reverend's gathering. If someone tries to pass a container over the cordon, seize it."

Lew's mouth flattened into something like a promise. "Yes, Detective."

Holloway cleared his throat, finding his mayor's voice. "Detective, I insist on counsel."

"You'll get to insist when the state arrives," Naomi said. "Until then, you'll answer my questions."

"We have rights," asserted Stone, the lobby man with the self-pressed hands. "You can't detain elected officials without charge."

Naomi didn't blink. "I can secure a crime scene with living witnesses and one dead one. You're welcome to test me."

Silence poured itself back over them.

She picked up the sign-in book again, read the strokes as if they were fingerprints. "Council entered between six thirty-six and six fifty-one. Staff at six ten. Custodian at six fifteen. Doors closed at six fifty-eight. Reed's visible symptoms began at seven seventeen. That gives our accomplice approximately a forty-five-minute or so window to prep his cup."

Cobb whispered, "Greg always brought his own. Said the tap gave him headaches."

Naomi turned on that sentence. "Always?"

"Always," Cobb said, and now her words carried memory rather than fear. "Sometimes he'd chuckle about it. 'If I die at a meeting,' he'd say, 'you'll all know I finally drank the town water.'" She covered her mouth again. "Dear Lord."

Les returned with a tablet. "East hall camera is flaky, like Ned said. It drops frames. But we got South Hall clean." He set the device on the table and cued a video. The council chamber door, time stamp ticking. Dwayne is entering with folders. Ned with a tool bag, shouldering the hinge. Reed was the first council member to arrive. Two more council members arrived with coats and briefcases. Then a figure in a dark coat, face obscured, carrying a tote. Unbranded. The kind of bag you pick up at a supermarket. The figure walked back out five minutes later, their face still obscured.

"Pause," she said. "Zoom."

Les pinched the image. The pixels resisted, then surrendered enough. The figure's stride was neither hurried nor furtive but confident, habitual. The hand not carrying the bag dangled a key ring. On the ring, something small and distinctive flashed once when it caught the hall light. It was a cross-shaped fob.

Cobb made a slight, helpless sound. "Reverend—"

"It's a cross," Naomi said, neutral, clinical. "Lots of people in this town wear crosses. The question is who walked into that hall at six forty-nine carrying a tote only to leave five minutes later.

Naomi pointed, "Someone had the access, the habit, the comfort level, and the practice to place cyanide in Reed's cup and make sure no one took notice of them. Someone who assumes authority fits like a coat. Someone who knows where the cameras break and where the hinges stick. Someone who prayed in the right pews and signed the right lines and told themselves it was for the town's good."

"Who?" Stone said, strangled.

Naomi didn't answer.

The medical examiner arrived with two techs and a zipped black bag that made Harriet Cobb sob again. The procedure unfolded. Photos were taken, swabs and tweezers were used, the cup was isolated, the hands were bagged, and a sheet was drawn.

While they worked, Naomi pulled James aside to the room's far corner, out of earshot but not out of sight. "When we let them go," she said, "they will run to Blake.

"We're letting them go?"

"After statements," she said.

James said. "You want me at Mae's when this breaks?"

"I want you where your words do the most damage to the right people," she said. "But hear me: they will come for you now. Not with guns. With rumors. With your past."

He met her eyes. "I told you my past."

"They'll tell it worse," she said, and for a moment her voice carried a human ache that wasn't strategy. "Stay close to me until the state arrives."

"That an order?" he asked, attempting lightness that didn't quite lift.

"Consider it a selfish request," she said. "I don't want to lose my best witness."

Naomi returned to the table. "We're taking brief statements now," she said. "Nothing long. Just where you were between six and seven, who you spoke to, and whether you touched anything not yours."

One by one, they answered, small, insufficient truths that sounded like rehearsed alibis. Dwayne stammered through his. Ned stuck to specifics like nails. Holloway wore the dignity of a man who had practiced it too much. Stone spoke to the table more than to Naomi. Teller just answered without twitching. Cobb clutched her pearls and said the Reverend taught her that confession without contrition is theater.

"Here is what happens next," she said. "You are escorted downstairs and released to your homes. You do not speak to the press. You do not convene with each other. You do not accept pastoral counsel. You wait for a call from my office or from the state, and when it comes, you answer."

"On what charge?" Stone whispered.

"On the charge," Naomi said, "of being alive in a room where a man died because he helped steal from his neighbors."

"Before you go," she said, "understand this. Elena Marquez did not act alone. Her accomplice has keys to this building, knows the hall where the camera fails, and knows the time when it is safe to enter without being noticed.

Every head turned toward the door, as if the door might confess.

Naomi's voice dropped to a hush that somehow carried more than any shout. "Her accomplice is here."

"Friends or foes," she said, repeating the vow she'd made to the room a half hour earlier, "I will know which you are by morning."

No one stood. For a heartbeat, they all stayed right where they were, as if movement might trigger something worse. Then, one by one, they rose and filed out.

Only James and Naomi remained. He picked up his notebook. She picked up the stack of statements. Outside, the prayer swelled and then broke off on a single syllable, as if a conductor had lifted a hand.

James looked at her. "You think they believed you?"

"I think they heard me," she said. "Belief is optional. Hearing is not."

They stepped into the night. The door swung shut behind them with a sound like a verdict reached and sealed.

Chapter 19 – The Warrant

The town's people moved quietly through the streets, their voices muted, their eyes lowered. Rumors traveled faster than the truth.

After Reed's poisoning, Reverend Samuel Blake preached twice as often. His sermons swelling with promises of "order through faith." The townsfolk listened. They wanted to believe him.

Naomi Pierce did not. She sat in the corner booth of Mae's Café, the curtains half drawn, a stack of worn files between her hands. "We're missing something," she said. "Something that ties them all together."

James Whitaker, across from her, looked just as worn. He'd stopped pretending to be objective somewhere around Victor Lane's death. "You mean besides the trail of bodies?"

She shot him a look. "Lane's death wasn't random. Neither was Reed's.

She reached into her coat and produced a small ledger, the one she'd retrieved weeks ago from the burned office downtown. "This," she said, tapping it. "It's more than just accounting. Look."

James leaned closer. The pages were lined with rows of figures, initials, and a repeating symbol, a simple cross drawn beside every fifth entry. He frowned. "You've been decoding this?"

She nodded. "Tried to. But the system's layered. The cross isn't just a mark. It's a multiplier. Each one shifts the numerical pattern."

James rubbed his jaw, scanning the faint lines. "It's encryption. Primitive, but deliberate."

"Lane handled numbers for half the town," Naomi said. "But someone had to design this. He wasn't clever enough to hide money this cleanly."

James turned a page. The handwriting changed halfway through. It was neater, practiced, and deliberate. "This second half looks different. Controlled."

Naomi's gaze hardened. "It's Blake's."

They spread the rest of the ledgers across the table. Mae had closed early, leaving the café dim except for the yellow glow of the pendant lamp. Naomi flipped open a municipal file, revealing scanned donation records. "Look at these names. Margaret Redmond. Elena Marquez. Evan Carlisle,Victor Lane. Each made 'donations' to St. Alban's Church within weeks of major business losses or investigations."

James leaned forward. "So they were funneling hush money through the church?"

"Exactly, and look at the withdrawal codes. Each one ends with the same letters—'S.B." Samuel Blake. Naomi's tone turned colder. "He was at the center of every transaction. He was a spiritual advisor, confidant, and silent collector. He used confession to gather information and guilt to turn it into profit."

James flipped to another page. There it was again. Dates aligning with every key death. Charles Redmond's murder. Margaret's drowning. Reed's poisoning. Even Lane's final withdrawal appeared two days before his assassination.

Naomi whispered, "He used their sins to trap them. When they wanted out, he offered salvation. For a price."

James nodded grimly. "And when the price wasn't enough, he buried them."

The name "Elena Marquez" appeared three times in the ledgers. Next to it, a notation: *Remittance for protection, $5,000 USD.*

Naomi stared at it. "He kept her paying even after she was arrested. Blake must be using the money to pay guards to keep her scared so she doesn't talk."

James's brow furrowed. "How? She's in county lockup."

"He has connections," Naomi said. "Blake visits the jail twice a month for 'pastoral care.' He's keeping her quiet. Elena believed she was avenging her mother," Naomi said quietly. "But Blake made her think Redmond's death was justice, not manipulation. She's protecting him even now."

She turned another page, revealing a final, unmarked entry. A wire transfer to a New Hampshire bank under a trust titled *The Ashwood Renewal Fund.*

By late evening, they left the café. James walked Naomi to her car.

"You think he knows we're close?" he asked.

Naomi rested her hands on the roof of her sedan, scanning the street. "He's too smart not to. But if he feels cornered, he'll get sloppy." Her gaze was distant. "Even zealots make mistakes. Especially when they think God's on their side."

James gave a thin smile. "Then let's give him a reason to pray."

James climbed the narrow stairs to his room above the café, exhaustion pressing behind his eyes. He laid the ledgers across his desk, spreading them like a map of corruption.

He didn't hear the knock at first. It was soft, almost polite, three measured taps.

He opened the door cautiously.

Reverend Samuel Blake stood in the hall, his collar gleaming white against his black coat. His expression was calm, his eyes patient. "Mr. Whitaker," he said warmly. "Forgive the intrusion. I thought we might talk."

"You've been busy, stirring the embers of tragedy. Some in this town think you mean well. I know better." Blake's eyes glinted. "You're a man who loves chaos because it gives you purpose. But chaos consumes good men, Mr. Whitaker. You've seen it."

James stepped closer. "You sent someone to kill Victor Lane."

"Lane chose his own end," Blake said. "Sin finds its balance."

James's voice sharpened. "And Redmond? Margaret, Reed? Elena? How many people have you used?"

Blake's tone softened, almost pitying. "Detective Pierce is infecting you with her skepticism. You mistake my guidance for control."

"I've seen some of our books."

The reverend's smile faltered for the first time. "You know those are sacred records of donations, tithes, acts of goodwill."

"They're blood money," James said. "You blackmailed your own congregation."

Blake's voice turned colder. "You think they want freedom from me? They want protection. They need someone to make sense of it all. You think Naomi can do that?"

"She can," James said. "And she will."

Blake's eyes narrowed. "You're standing in a storm you can't survive, son. For the good of this town, walk away."

James met his gaze. "I'm not your son."

Blake gave a slight nod, as if in benediction. "Then I'll pray for you anyway." He turned and left, his footsteps slow and deliberate. The scent of incense lingered long after he was gone.

Naomi arrived before dawn. She found James at his desk, staring at the ledgers.

"He was here," James said quietly. "Blake."

Her eyes widened. "When?"

"Last night. Said he came to offer prayer."

Naomi's jaw clenched. "He's baiting you."

"He's warning us. He knows about the ledgers we have."

She crossed the room and placed a steady hand on his shoulder. "Then we use them while we still can.I contacted a judge that I worked with on previous cases. He issues a search warrant for Blake's office

He looked up. "You mean tonight?"

"I mean now," she said. "If he's moving to cover his tracks, the church records are next. We find the originals before he burns them."

St. Alban's Chapel, with its stained-glass windows glowed faintly from candlelight, the colors distorted by mist.

They went to the side door that led into the chapel offices. Naomi knocked and announced herself. There was no answer. The door was unlocked so they entered and turned on the lights. The scent of wax and old wood filled the air.

Blake's office consisted of a polished desk with neatly stacked papers, pictures and a crucifix on the wall.

"Remember, this warrant serves only this office. Don't wander outside of it."

Naomi worked quickly, pulling open drawers."Everything's too clean," she said. "He's scrubbed this place."

James noticed a cabinet marked *Archives.* The lock was old and open. Inside were only notes on some of the parishioners. Behind a picture on the wall they found an old pick lock safe. They were able to get it open and inside found a stack of older ledgers, bound in leather and tied with twine.

Naomi untied the top one. Inside were rows of numbers and notations matching those from Lane's files, but these were intact. Full names. Dates.

James pointed to an entry: *Payment received—E. Marquez (facility donation).* The rest were town officials and business owners. He's built an empire on guilt."

Before they could gather everything, a faint creak echoed from the hallway.

Footsteps. Slow. Even. Confident. Whoever it was walked past the office and down the hall.

"I made a copy of the warrant. We have to leave it with a note that it was served. Also a list of items we removed from the office.She put them on the desk.

They gathered up the ledgers and left the chapel the way they had come in.The night air hit them like cold breath as they stepped into the fog.

Back at the café, Naomi locked the ledgers in her briefcase. "We have enough," she said. "Financials, transactions, direct ties. Tomorrow we plan on how to break him.

James rubbed his eyes. "You think that'll stop him?"

"It'll break his hold," she said. "You expose a man like that to light, he burns."

He nodded slowly. "Then tomorrow, we burn him."

Naomi gave a tired but resolute smile. "Get some sleep, Whitaker. You'll want to be awake when Ashwood's god falls."

James stood at the window long after she'd gone, thinking and wondering how it would affect the town. Somewhere inside the chapel, he imagined Blake kneeling in prayer. Not to repent, but to prepare.

And for the first time, James wondered if even truth could survive what was coming.

Chapter 20 – The Trap

The fog refused to lift from Ashwood. It hung like gauze over the rooftops, swallowing sound and shape, as if the town were holding its breath after the night in the council chamber. The morning papers told half the story: Councilman Found Dead During Emergency Session. What they didn't tell was how deep the rot ran—or who was next.

Naomi read the article once, folded it neatly, and dropped it into the wastebasket beside her desk. "They're already rewriting the truth," she said.

James sat across from her, rubbing a thumb along his jaw. "Let them. They'll print whatever Blake tells them until we give them something better."

Naomi's eyes flicked up, calm but sharp. "You're suggesting bait."

He nodded. "You said it yourself. Fear flushes the guilty faster than truth."

She leaned back, considering. "A trap, then."

"A lie that looks too good to ignore," James said. "If Blake's people are still cleaning up, they'll move fast on anything that smells like exposure—or money."

Naomi turned toward the board on the wall. Red string stretched between the names of Redmond, Elena, Margaret, Lane, and Blake. Reed's photo now hung beneath them with a black pin.

"Money," she murmured. "It always comes back to that. If we make them believe something valuable survived—something that can burn them—they'll take the bait. Then we wait and watch who bites."

Naomi glanced over her shoulder. "You think you can sell the story?"

"I am a journalist," he said. "Lies are just stories with better timing."

They built the lie in quiet layers. Naomi let it slip to a sergeant that a sealed evidence box had been recovered from Lane's office before the fire—a box containing documents about hidden money buried on Redmond's estate. And that, tomorrow morning, the property would be searched until it was found. By noon, whispers had reached every corner of Ashwood. By dusk, the whispers sounded like fact.

James had done his part, too. He "accidentally" mentioned it to Mae while buying coffee. Several customers heard. Mae's reaction—half disbelief, half curiosity—was exactly what he needed. Within an hour, he overheard a customer say, "They found where the old man's treasure is, you hear? Buried somewhere on his estate."

By sunset, the bait was set.

Naomi stood at her office window, watching fog drift through the square. "You realize," she said quietly, "that if this works, someone could die tonight."

James met her eyes. "Someone already has. Four times over."

She didn't argue. Instead, she opened her desk drawer and pulled out a small metal key. "This gets us through the east gate of Redmond's property. Less visibility from the main road."

He took it, feeling the cold metal against his palm. "What happens if no one shows?"

"Then we wait until they do," she said.

The estate had an abandoned look. What had once been manicured gardens were now overgrown and wild. The pavilion still stood, streaked with moss, its benches slick with dew.

James and Naomi moved through the fog like ghosts. She wore dark clothes, her badge tucked away, her hair pulled back.

He carried his notebook and a flashlight, its beam dimmed beneath a strip of cloth.

James checked his watch. "Almost midnight." He glanced toward the tree line. "You think Blake will come himself?"

"No," she said. "Men like him don't dirty their hands. He'll send someone loyal enough to die for him."

They settled into the shadows near the pavilion, behind a low wall swallowed by ivy. Time stretched thin. The fog thickened until the world seemed reduced to two sounds—their breathing and the slow drip of water from the fountain.

At last, a faint crunch of gravel broke the silence. A flashlight beam cut through the mist, wavering, then steadying. The figure that emerged was hunched against the cold, wrapped in a long coat and hat. He moved with purpose, not caution, as though he already knew exactly where to look.

Naomi's whisper barely stirred the air. "There."

When the man lifted his head, the beam caught his features, and James's stomach dropped. "Councilman Stone."

Naomi's eyes widened. She moved first, rising from the shadows. "Stone. Stop right there. Police!"

Stone froze, then straightened slowly. His voice cracked. "You don't understand. I had to—"

"Turn around," Naomi ordered. "Hands visible."

Stone shook his head, voice trembling. "It's bigger than Elena. She wasn't leading—she was following orders."

Naomi took a cautious step forward. "Whose orders?"

Stone opened his mouth. But the answer never came.

The gunshot cracked through the fog—sharp and final. Stone's chest jerked, and he dropped to his knees before collapsing.

James hit the ground, dragging Naomi down with him behind the stone wall. A second shot splintered the edge of the pavilion post inches from his shoulder.

"Sniper!" Naomi hissed. She drew her weapon, scanning the tree line. "Do you see him?"

James strained to listen. Nothing but the fading echo of the shot. Whoever fired was already moving—or gone.

Naomi crawled toward Stone's body, keeping low. She pressed two fingers to his neck, then shook her head. "Dead."

James crouched beside her, heart hammering. "Same precision as Lane. Clean. Deliberate."

"He was silenced," Naomi said, her voice low but steady. "Whoever's left is erasing every loose thread."

James followed her gaze toward the trees. "Which means the trap worked. But he died before we got any more information."

They searched what little ground they could under cover of darkness, finding only faint impressions of footprints in the wet soil leading toward the old service road. The pattern was distinct—heavy boots, military tread, deliberate stride.

"Professional," Naomi murmured. "Not random muscle. Someone trained."

James knelt, tracing the impression with his flashlight. "Could be hired help. Could be—"

He stopped, his beam catching something glinting in the mud. A bullet casing. He picked it up carefully. ".308 Winchester. High-powered rifle. Two hundred yards, easy."

Naomi nodded grimly. "He shot from the ridge above the orchard. Perfect angle. Clean escape route."

They stood in silence, the fog closing around them like a curtain.

James stared down at Stone's body. "He was trying to tell us something."

They loaded Stone into the coroner's van themselves, refusing to leave it to the patrol officers who arrived minutes later.

Naomi gave curt orders, her voice clipped, her face unreadable.

When the van drove off, she leaned against the hood of her car, arms crossed. "We just lost a man who could name the leader."

In the morning, at Mae's café, dawn thinned the fog into pale strands. The air smelled of coffee and rain. Mae stood behind the counter, her apron dusted with flour. "You look like you've seen a ghost," she said.

"Close enough," James replied.

Mae poured coffee into two mugs, her movements slow and deliberate. "There's talk already. People are saying Stone's ghost is wandering near the orchard. Folks love making legends out of tragedies."

"Let them talk," Naomi said. "It'll keep Blake guessing how much we know."

Mae set the cups down. "And how much do you know?"

Naomi hesitated. "Enough to know we're outnumbered."

Mae nodded, wiping her hands. "Then maybe stop playing defense."

James met her eyes. "Meaning?"

"Stop chasing shadows," she said. "Start shining lights."

Naomi gave a small smile. "We're working on that."

Later, in James's room above the café, they sat by the window and watched the fog lift in thin strands from the street. The quiet felt heavier now, filled with the ghosts of what they couldn't prove.

James broke the silence. "He said she wasn't leading—she was following orders."

Naomi didn't answer right away. "Then we find who gave the order." She turned the bullet casing over in her hand, its brass surface catching the light. "Someone who owns God in this town," she said finally. "Someone who built the church, paid for the council campaigns, and convinced everyone they were acting out of duty, not greed."

James stared out the window. "And now we know Stone was killed for trying to tell us." His jaw tightened. "You think Blake knew that we would be there?"

"He knows everything that happens in Ashwood," Naomi said. "But tonight, we learned something too."

"What's that?"

She met his gaze. "He's afraid."

James gave a grim smile. "Good. Fear makes people sloppy."

Naomi looked out toward the fog-drenched hills. "Then we'll use it. One more trap—but this time, he won't see it coming."

Her words hung between them like a vow.

Somewhere in the distance, thunder rolled low across the sky, and the lights of Ashwood flickered as if the town itself were bracing for what came next.

Chapter 21 – The Cost of the Trap

The day dawned colder than anyone expected. A thin frost glazed the square, catching the early light in sharp, uneven reflections. By midmorning, the town of Ashwood was awake but uneasy.

The news had spread fast: Detective Naomi Pierce was calling a public council session at Town Hall, open to citizens and the press. Rumor said it wasn't about the Relief Fund anymore. Rumor said it was about the Reverend.

From his room above Mae's Café, James Whitaker watched as people gathered in tight knots near the steps. There were business owners, council members, families, and parishioners. Some came clutching prayer books, others folded newspapers.

Mae caught him at the door with a cup of coffee. "They'll eat her alive if she doesn't have proof," she warned softly.

"She's got more than proof," James said. "She's got the truth."

Mae shook her head. "Truth doesn't always win, Whitaker. Sometimes it just bleeds slower."

He gave her a tired smile. "Then let's hope it bleeds in the right direction."

Inside Town Hall, the air was heavy with expectation. Every seat was filled. Reporters lined the back wall, notebooks poised.

Reverend Samuel Blake sat near the front, flanked by two church elders. He wore his collar and a calm, practiced smile. To anyone watching, he looked like a man at peace.

Naomi Pierce entered without ceremony, a leather briefcase in hand. Her expression was controlled, but her eyes burned with focus. "Thank you for coming," she began. "This session is being recorded for the public record."

Mayor Addison Holloway cleared his throat. "Detective Pierce, may I remind you this is a civil hearing, not a criminal proceeding."

"I'm aware," Naomi said. "But what's discussed today may change both."

Whispers rippled through the room.

James stood near the back, pen in hand, though he wasn't writing. He was watching faces, noting which ones went pale, and watching hands to see who was nervous when Naomi opened her case.

"Over the past two months," Naomi said, "Ashwood has experienced a string of deaths, all connected by proximity to Charles Redmond's financial network. Those deaths include Charles himself, Margaret Redmond, Gregory Reed, Victor Lane and Councilman Stone. Evidence links them through falsified transactions and coded ledgers that trace back to one institution." She lifted a ledger from her briefcase and placed it on the table with a quiet thud. "St. Alban's Church."

The room erupted in noise. Voices overlapped, chairs scraped, and one of the elders muttered a prayer under his breath.

When the noise subsided, Naomi continued. "These ledgers document donations and 'relief payments' redirected through a series of shell accounts. The final beneficiary is listed under the initials

'S.B.,' verified against Reverend Blake's own signature on multiple financial authorizations."

She turned the ledger toward the crowd. "This isn't faith. It's fraud."

Blake rose slowly, a calm shadow among the chaos. His voice carried easily. "Detective Pierce, you're mistaken. Those are church records, charitable funds for the needy. You've taken them out of context."

Naomi's tone stayed even. "So the needy included convicted embezzlers, blackmailed council members, and a detective now serving time for homicide?"

A murmur swept the room, Elena's name whispered like a ghost.

Blake's composure faltered briefly. "You're twisting this into blasphemy. You think you can understand the purpose behind every soul I tried to save?"

James could see the shift happening, the Reverend's voice rising from calm persuasion into something darker.

Naomi met his gaze without flinching. "I don't pretend to understand salvation, Reverend. But I know extortion when I see it. And I know blackmail when I read it."

She held up a printed record. "Bank statements show direct transfers from Redmond's estate to your personal account. Funds disguised as restoration grants. You bled this town dry under the guise of redemption."

A gasp came from the back. Someone whispered, "He saved my sister's house." Another voice said, "He took our savings."

Blake spread his hands like a preacher before the pulpit. "Yes, I took money. To build, to preserve, to protect this town from its own corruption. Redmond, Reed, Lane—they were thieves, every one of them. I simply redirected their greed toward grace."

Naomi said quietly, "Grace doesn't leave bodies behind."

The mayor's gavel struck. "Order!"

But the crowd wouldn't settle. Some shouted in outrage, others in defense. The church elders looked ready to faint.

Naomi stepped back from the table, giving Blake room to speak. "You have a chance to explain," she said. "Why did you threaten those who stopped paying?"

Blake's eyes narrowed. "Because faith demands obedience." His tone had lost its practiced softness. He turned toward the crowd. "You think I wanted this? You think I enjoyed watching our town rot while you all looked away? I gave you order when you begged for peace! I carried your sins!"

James could feel it—the unmasking, the calm veneer cracking to reveal the man beneath.

Naomi said quietly, "And when those sins stopped paying dividends?"

Blake's voice thundered. "Then they had no more use to the Lord!"

The chamber fell silent. Even Blake seemed startled by the force of his own voice.

"Your sermons preach forgiveness," Naomi said. "But your partnerships end in graves."

Blake's mask slipped completely then. His voice dropped to a near whisper, the kind that filled the silence like poison.

"You think you can save them from me? They came willingly. They wanted someone to lead them. I gave them purpose."

Naomi's tone stayed cold. "You used their guilt to make yourself untouchable."

"You call it guilt," he said, "but it's faith that built this town. You, Detective—you and your cynicism—you'd tear it down just to stand on the ashes and call yourself righteous."

"Truth doesn't destroy," Naomi said. "Lies do."

"Then let's see what your truth buys you."

He moved suddenly, snatching a folded paper from his coat and throwing it onto the table. "This is my account of what happened. Signed confessions from the very people you defend. Read them. Redmond's pride. Margaret's indifference. Elena's vengeance. Reed's greed. Lane and Stone's cowardice. Every sin accounted for."

He pointed toward the ledger. "You think that book damns me? It absolves me. Every name in there asked to be judged."

Naomi's reply was quiet but firm. "You're not their god."

For a long moment, neither spoke. Then Blake smiled again, the mask settling back into place. "No," he said softly. "But I was the only one willing to play him."

The mayor's gavel struck again. "Reverend Blake, you're under formal investigation. Detective Pierce, please surrender those documents to the clerk's custody."

Naomi nodded. "No,sir. These go to the state 's further investigation."

Uniformed officers moved forward to escort him from the room. But as Blake stepped into the aisle, he turned to face the crowd. "You're all complicit!" he shouted. "You paid me to wash your hands clean, and now you condemn me for doing it! You wanted your sins forgotten. Now you'll choke on them!"

The officers pulled him back, but the damage was done.

The room fractured into chaos—yells, sobs, shouts for mercy or explanation. Some rose to leave, while others shouted over one another, demanding that Naomi arrest him on the spot.

Through it all, Blake laughed. A soft, chilling laugh that carried long after he was gone.

Outside, the crowd had gathered. Reporters swarmed, cameras flashing as officers led Blake down the steps. He didn't resist. He walked like a man attending his own sermon, hands folded, head high.

"Reverend! Is it true you embezzled church funds?"

"Were you involved in the Redmond murder?"

"Do you have anything to say to your congregation?"

Blake stopped at the bottom step and raised his hands. "My only sin," he said, "was believing I could save a godless town."

The press went wild. The crowd's anger broke into shouts. Someone threw a rock; it shattered against a police cruiser.

By late afternoon, the square had emptied. Only scraps of newspaper and broken tape fluttered across the ground.

Naomi sat on the courthouse steps, exhaustion finally catching up with her. James joined her with two cups of coffee from Mae's, both lukewarm.

"You did it," he said quietly. "You broke him."

She gave a faint smile. "Men like that don't break. They bend. Then they come back sharper."

James took a sip of coffee. "He's in custody. The state will take over from here."

Naomi stared toward the horizon, where the church bell tower stood dark against the fading light. "I've seen too many men of power talk their way out of chains."

"Then we make sure he doesn't."

She turned to him. "You staying?"

He hesitated. "For now. Someone needs to write this down right."

Naomi smirked. "Just don't make me sound like a hero."

"Wouldn't dream of it."

They sat in silence for a long time.

When the first stars appeared, Naomi finally stood. "Tomorrow's the press release. And then..."

"And then?"

"Blake said I was wrong, that it doesn't end with him. Maybe he was lying. Maybe not. But men like him don't build alone."

That night, long after the square went quiet, James stood at his window and looked toward the church. The steeple was dark now, but something flickered inside—a faint candle glow, steady and deliberate.

Someone was still there.

He thought of Blake's words, of the calm certainty in his voice when he said: *You think this ends with me. You're wrong.*

James closed his notebook and whispered into the still air, "Then we'll find the rest of you."

Outside, the candle in the church guttered once, then went out.

Chapter 22 – The Last Confession

The rain began before dawn. Thin and cold, it fell in whispering sheets across Ashwood, running in silver streams down the courthouse steps and pooling in the square where, only a day before, Reverend Samuel Blake had been paraded before cameras and questions.

By morning, he was gone. He had escaped.

Naomi Pierce stood in the sheriff's office, her jaw tight as she stared at the open holding cell.

The deputy, pale beneath the fluorescent light said " The cameras went dead at two fifteen."

James Whitaker entered, rainwater dripping from his coat. "They found a van abandoned outside town. The driver's missing. He had help."

Naomi questioned the guard, who insisted he had not left the office but had felt suddenly sick after drinking some coffee. "I must have passed out—and when I woke up, the cell was empty."

Naomi rubbed her forehead. "He's heading somewhere familiar. Somewhere with meaning."

"The church?"

She shook her head. "Too obvious. He knows we'd start there."

James's gaze drifted to the map pinned to the wall. He studied it for a moment, then said quietly, "Then where does a man like Blake go when the world finally sees him for what he is?"

Naomi followed his gaze. After a beat, they spoke at the same time.

"The Redmond Mill."

It made terrible sense. The old textile plant had been shuttered for a decade, its foundations rotting into the marsh. It was where Redmond's fortune had begun—and where Blake's sermons of salvation had first reached the workers.

"Symbolic," James murmured. "He started his empire there."

Naomi strapped her sidearm on. "Then that's where we finish it."

The drive through the outskirts of Ashwood felt endless. Rain blurred the road ahead, turning the landscape into streaks of gray and brown. The forest pressed close on either side, branches skeletal and black against the sky.

James stared out the passenger window. "You think he planned this?"

Naomi's hands tightened on the wheel. "He plans everything. But even he can't control the endgame."

"He's not the kind to go quietly," James said.

"I'm counting on it."

They reached the mill by dusk. The structure loomed, dilapidated, its windows shattered and walls mottled with mildew. The tall chimney leaned slightly, a dying monument to Ashwood's industrial past.

Naomi cut the headlights. "He'll see us coming if we use light."

James slipped his flashlight into his pocket but left it off. "I'll follow your lead."

"Stay close," she said. "And if he runs, don't be a hero."

He gave a faint smile. "You know I never listen."

"Unfortunately, yes."

They entered through a rusted side door. The hinges screeched, echoing through the cavernous space beyond. Inside, the air was damp and thick with decay. Machinery stood like hulking shadows—silent, skeletal relics of another age.

Somewhere above, a faint clatter broke the silence.

Naomi signaled for James to stay low. They moved toward the sound, weaving through rusted catwalks and broken stairwells.

A voice floated down from the darkness. "Detective Pierce. Mr. Whitaker. You should have stayed home."

Blake stood on the upper walkway, silhouetted against a broken window that bled gray light. His collar was gone, his shirt torn, his hands streaked with grime—but his eyes burned with the same terrible calm.

"You think you've won," he said. "You think the town will thank you for destroying its faith?"

Naomi raised her weapon. "It's not faith I'm after. It's justice."

"Justice?" Blake's laugh echoed through the rafters. "You wouldn't know justice if I preached it to you."

He began to pace along the walkway. "I built this town's conscience. Every sinner came to me begging to be cleansed. I took their guilt, their filth, and turned it into something holy."

"By killing them?" Naomi said.

"I didn't kill anyone," Blake said. "They killed themselves—slowly, willingly. I just showed them the path."

James stepped forward. "You turned their weaknesses into profit."

Blake's eyes locked on him. "You're a writer, aren't you, Mr. Whitaker? You of all people should understand. Every good story needs a martyr."

The floor above them creaked. Naomi gestured toward a metal stairway, and they began to climb, their steps careful and deliberate. Rain hammered the roof, echoing like distant drums.

As they reached the landing, Blake moved deeper into the mill, his voice rising over the storm.

"Do you know why Elena Marquez trusted me? Because I told her the truth. I told her her father's money came from exploitation, from broken backs and silenced protests. She needed someone to justify her vengeance. I obliged."

Naomi's eyes narrowed. "You made her your weapon."

"I made her useful," Blake said. "The girl wanted redemption. I gave her purpose. She'll die believing she served something greater than herself."

"But she's alive," Naomi said sharply. "And she's talking."

That stopped him—for just a moment.

Then he smiled again. "She'll talk herself into circles. Without me, she's nothing."

"Without you," Naomi said, "she's free from your influence."

Blake backed toward a platform overlooking the mill floor. His voice softened, almost gentle.

"You two think you're different. Do you think exposing me changes anything? This town needs men like me. Without faith, they'll tear each other apart."

He laughed softly. "You don't understand. You can't just wash away sin. It stains everything."

Naomi advanced another step. "You've said enough, Reverend. It's over."

Blake looked at her calmly. "You think so?"

He turned and fired. The shot cracked through the air, deafening in the hollow space. Naomi dropped behind a support beam as glass shattered overhead.

"James!"

"I'm fine!"

Blake fired again, the bullet sparking off metal. "You think you can stop me?" he shouted. "I am Ashwood! Everything you touch here belongs to me!"

Naomi leaned out, returning fire. The shot struck a beam inches from his shoulder. He ducked, moving toward a catwalk along the far wall.

"Go left!" Naomi yelled.

James darted toward the stairwell, circling wide to cut him off. The old boards groaned underfoot, every sound amplified in the cavernous space.

Blake fired again, missing wide. His aim was unsteady now—panic replacing purpose.

Naomi climbed the last few steps and leveled her weapon. "Drop it, Blake!"

He turned, breathing hard, the gun trembling in his hand. "You don't understand. If I fall, they all fall. This town will rot!"

Naomi's voice remained steady. "Maybe it's time it grew something new."

He pulled the trigger. Click. Empty.

Naomi fired. The bullet struck his shoulder, spinning him backward. He hit the railing, staggered—and slipped.

James lunged forward, catching his arm before he fell.

For a moment, they hung there, Blake's weight dragging James toward the edge. Naomi grabbed James's jacket, anchoring him.

"Don't let go!" she shouted.

Blake's grip tightened. His eyes met James's—wild, desperate, pleading. "You can't let me die," he whispered.

James pulled him upward, dragging him back onto the platform. Blake collapsed, gasping, his face ashen.

Naomi moved quickly, cuffing his wrists. "It's over."

Blake looked up at her, his expression curiously serene. "You think you've saved them," he said. "But when the next serpent comes, they'll beg for another shepherd."

Naomi stood, breathing hard. "Then they'll find one who doesn't bleed them dry."

By dawn, the mill swarmed with state police. The storm had broken, leaving mist rising from the wet ground. Blake sat on the back of an ambulance, his arm bandaged, his eyes distant.

Naomi stood nearby, arms crossed. "He'll be transported to the hospital, then to county detention," a trooper said. "Charges will follow."

Naomi nodded. "Make sure he's never left alone."

James watched as Blake was loaded into the van. The Reverend caught his eye briefly and smiled—faint, knowing, resigned.

When the doors shut, James exhaled. "You think that's really the end?"

Naomi didn't answer right away. "It's the end of him. Not the damage he did."

They walked back toward her car. The sun broke through the fog, casting pale gold across the ruined mill.

Weeks later, the town began to heal. St. Alban's Church closed its doors until a new preacher could be found. The state seized the Relief Fund for redistribution. Mae's Café stayed open later than ever, the air lighter, no longer heavy with unspoken fear.

James's articles ran in three major papers under the title Ashwood Unmasked. He didn't name every name. Some wounds were better left to heal quietly—but the story became a warning about power and faith twisted too far.

Naomi remained as lead investigator for the regional task force. She tracked those still affected by Blake's influence and arranged counseling for those who needed it.

James and Naomi met often. Sometimes over coffee at Mae's, sometimes in his apartment, talking about what Ashwood might become now that the truth had surfaced.

"Still chasing ghosts?" he asked her once.

"Always," she said. "But at least now I know who's watching."

Chapter 23 – The Aftermath

Ashwood was quiet again. Too quiet. The kind of quiet that settles over a town after it's been emptied of its secrets. The rain had stopped days ago, leaving the streets washed clean, but the people still moved as though they were stepping through the wreckage of something unseen.

In the weeks after Reverend Blake's arrest, the town tried to resume its rhythm. The square reopened, and the café filled with conversation again. But every smile carried a question, and every handshake lingered a second too long, as if searching for hidden intent.

Naomi Pierce stayed behind to finalize her reports and hand over Blake's case to the state prosecutors. He was transferred to a secure facility upstate. His trial would come later, but for now, the people of Ashwood could breathe.

The sheriff's office didn't stay empty long. The town needed stability—someone untainted by the chaos that had nearly consumed them. The council, still weary from the scandal, voted unanimously to bring in Sheriff Walter Briggs, a man nearing retirement who had spent decades working homicide in Philadelphia.

Briggs arrived with little fanfare. He was tall, silver-haired, with a slow gait and eyes that had seen enough darkness to know when to stop chasing it.

When James first met him, Briggs stood outside the café with a steaming mug in hand, watching the morning settle over the square.

"You must be the journalist," Briggs said without turning.

James smiled faintly. "That's what they tell me."

Briggs took a sip of coffee. "Heard you stirred up quite a storm here."

"Depends who you ask," James said.

Briggs chuckled. "I like a town where the biggest excitement is a bake sale. But they tell me Ashwood needed steady hands."

"Probably true," James said. "You planning to stay long?"

"Until they don't need me anymore," Briggs said simply. "Then I'll find a lake somewhere and forget what sirens sound like."

James nodded, studying the older man. There was something grounding about him—no ambition, no hunger for power. Just quiet endurance.

"You'll do fine here," James said.

Briggs smiled faintly. "From what I've seen, you already did."

A week later, James made his way to the Whitaker estate—the place where everything had started. The engagement party, the death of Charles Redmond, the unraveling of Ashwood's carefully built illusions.

The gates stood open now, the grounds overgrown with early spring weeds. Hannah Moore, his cousin—once bright and full of optimism—had taken to living there again, though without the wedding that was meant to happen.

She met him on the porch, her expression soft but guarded.

They sat on the steps, the air carrying the scent of damp wood and lilacs. The estate loomed behind them like a relic—tired, but still standing.

"I've been trying to fix things up," Hannah said after a moment. "Not just the house. Me too, I guess."

James glanced at her. "You don't have to fix everything."

"I know. But I need something to do." She smiled faintly. "People still look at me like I was part of it. Redmond... Daniel... all of it."

James sighed. "That'll fade. People always need someone to blame when they're scared."

She turned to him. "And what about you? You're leaving, aren't you?"

He hesitated. "Yeah. There's a paper in Boston interested in what I've been writing. Might be good to get back to city noise."

"Running away again?" she teased gently.

"Maybe," he admitted. "But this time I'm not sure what I'm running from."

Hannah looked out over the field. "I think Ashwood's finally starting to heal, James. It's strange... knowing we survived all that."

He followed her gaze, the evening light touching the edges of the estate in gold. "You'll make this place whole again," he said. "You always did like impossible projects."

She laughed softly. "Maybe that runs in the family."

When he stood to leave, she caught his sleeve. "You did the right thing," she said quietly. "Even when it cost you."

James gave her a tired smile. "The right thing usually does." He gave her a big hug and said, "I won't stay away for so long. I'll keep in touch."

He left her standing on the porch, framed by the fading light—a survivor in a house full of ghosts.

Back in town, the changes were slow but visible. The church was shuttered, its windows boarded. A sign posted by the council read: Property Under State Investigation. The square felt busier now, the shadows shorter. Mae's café had become an unofficial town hall, where gossip had been replaced—at least for now—by cautious optimism.

Naomi sat in her usual booth, paperwork spread before her, a cup of untouched coffee cooling at her elbow.

James slid into the opposite seat. "You always work this much, or is Ashwood just lucky?"

Naomi smirked. "Occupational hazard. If I stop moving, I start overthinking."

He nodded toward the papers. "Blake's trial prep?"

"Mostly. They've got enough to bury him twice over."

"Good," James said quietly. "He deserves worse."

Naomi looked up. "You still writing about him?"

"Finished the last piece yesterday," he said. "It's strange. When I started, I thought I wanted to expose everything. Now I just want people to remember."

"That's enough," she said. "Memory keeps the next monster from crawling out of the dark."

He studied her for a moment. The lines of exhaustion around her eyes had softened, but the tension hadn't fully left.

"You ever think about slowing down?" he asked.

She raised an eyebrow. "And do what? Start a garden?"

He smiled. "Could be worse. I hear Briggs is looking for company fishing."

Naomi laughed—a rare, genuine sound. "I'd scare the fish away."

They sat in silence for a while, the hum of the café filling the space between them. Outside, the fog that had haunted Ashwood for months had finally lifted, replaced by a pale blue sky.

"I got an offer," Naomi said at last.

James looked up. "Promotion?"

"Transfer. There's a town dealing with a kidnapping and a murder case. They need help."

She gathered her papers. "If I take it, I could use someone who knows how to read people—and isn't afraid to ask questions."

"You mean someone who makes you sound like a hero," he teased.

"Hardly," she said. "Someone who knows when to call out the truth."

James stood. "Then consider this my official application."

Naomi looked at him for a long moment, then extended her hand.

He took it. The moment was steady, warm, unspoken.

Later that evening, James walked through the square one last time. Lamplight glowed gold on the damp cobblestones. He paused at the edge of the churchyard, where the steeple rose dark against the twilight. The boards creaked faintly in the wind, but there was no movement inside now—no flicker of candlelight, no whispered sermons.

He thought of Elena—alive, but changed. Of Hannah rebuilding her life. Of Naomi, already preparing to chase the next storm.

Ashwood was no longer a town defined by secrets. It was a town learning how to live without them.

Mae's voice called from behind him. "Leaving tonight, Whitaker?"

He turned to see her standing in the café doorway, wiping her hands on a towel.

"First thing in the morning," he said.

"You'll be back," she said. "People like you never stay gone."

"Maybe," he said. "But I hope when I do, there's less to write about."

Mae smiled. "For your sake, I hope not. You're too restless to retire."

He laughed softly. "Maybe so."

She tilted her head toward the window, where Naomi still sat inside, finishing her notes. "That one's the same way. You two will be chasing ghosts till you drop."

"Maybe," he said again, and went upstairs to pack.

Morning came quickly. He loaded his car and mapped out his route to Boston.

Footsteps approached behind him.

Naomi.

"You're early," he said.

"Couldn't sleep," she admitted. "Figured I'd see you off."

He smiled. "You get the transfer?"

She nodded. "They want me right away so I'm off to a town called North Ashford later today."

He studied her face. "You're really doing it."

"I am." She paused. "And I meant what I said. If you're serious, call me when your Boston job wraps up."

James met her eyes. "Count me in. I think we make a decent team."

Naomi smirked. "You mean when you're not breaking into crime scenes ahead of me."

"Occupational overlap," he said.

Naomi extended her hand again. "Take care of yourself, Whitaker."

He ignored the hand and folded her into an embrace. "You too... Naomi."

He got into his car and watched her through the windshield until she disappeared from view.

I'll miss you Naomi Pierce, he thought.

For the first time in a long while, James Whitaker didn't feel like he was running away.

He was moving forward.